# ZODIAC LOVERS

Paranormal Romance

Book One

AQUARIUS ✳ PISCES ✳ ARIES

**LANCE TAUBOLD**

Print and Digital Editions
Copyright 2018
Discover new and exciting works published by Invoke Books at
InvokeBooks.com

# DEDICATION

FOR RICHIE

MY INSPIRATION FOR THESE STORIES WITH LOVE

# TABLE OF CONTENTS

# AQUARIUS

Aquarius—The Water Bearer

Traits: Friendly, honest, loyal, original, independent, humanitarian, unpredictable, detached, intelligent, like to dream and plan for the future. When they find a life partner they can risk everything for them.

The nude man lying on the beach appeared to be dead.

The tropical storm, which had started late that afternoon, had gained in force considerably over the past several hours. The wind and rain now mercilessly assaulted the island. Lane, flashlight in hand, approached the body slowly, partly from the force of the winds, partly from fear.

The body was awash with seaweed, sand, and God knew what else. It was facedown. The head turned toward the ocean. Lane carefully knelt down and touched the body. It was still warm. Wet, but warm. Lane thought, and blew out a sigh of relief. At least he's not dead,. He turned the man over and tried to raise his head. The body was limp. Lane shoved the flashlight into the pocket of his shorts and struggled to get his arms beneath the body in the sand. The rain whipped at his face, as he managed to slowly lift up the man and get him into a standing position. The man was well muscled, yet trim—170 pounds or so— and Lane wriggled him into a carry-able position in his arms.

Lane slogged his way back to the house as the rain pelted and stung his face and torso. He regretted not at least putting on a shirt before venturing out. His rain-slicked body and the man's body kept sliding off one another, which made the steps going up to the deck even more difficult, so he climbed them slowly. Fortunately, there were only five steps and were very well secured.

Lane mentally patted himself on the back. He'd picked the perfect spot to build his island home so that he didn't have to build too high up or too far from the beach. Leeward side. Little wind and rain. Except, of course, during a storm. Still, his house would be safe enough. He was protected by a promontory not too far away, and he only got the aftermath and not the full brunt of the storm.

He set the man up against the door frame and maneuvered a hand behind him to open the door. The screen door lashed backwards with a slam as Lane shifted the man inside. He kicked the inside door closed and scooped the man into his arms once again. He'd worry about the screen door later. Sooner than later. That banging was going to drive him crazy.

Earlier, he'd gone outside to make sure everything was secured and safe on his deck. He'd noticed debris flying around. There had been splinters of wood and pieces of what looked like sailcloth. His examination of the debris revealed that it was, indeed, boat remains. Next step: go see if there was a wrecked boat nearby. That's when he'd stumbled upon the man.

Now, on his way through the house and back to his bedroom, Lane wondered if there was anyone else out there. After he'd checked out the man for injuries, he would go back and look. He trudged along carefully because there was only candlelight, and not much of that. He had turned on the small generator earlier in the evening for his refrigerator, but didn't want to drain it too much by the addition of lighting. In hindsight, the extra lighting would have been useful.

He entered the dimly lit room—one dim candle—and set the man down onto his bed. The man was breathing normally and didn't appear to have any major injuries or bleeding—at least from what he could see in the minimal lighting. He began to remove the seaweed and leaves from the man's head and face. The man stirred a little but did not wake up.

Lane pulled out his flashlight and scanned the body to ascertain if there were any cuts he'd missed. He now became aware of just how beautiful the man was. He had short cropped, dark blond hair, similar to his own he noted; sleek, taut muscles; a flat stomach; broad shoulders; a well-defined chest; muscular legs; and how could he not notice a good-sized male organ? Lane could feel his own male organ begin to stir. But then, what did he expect? It had been almost three years since he had been with a man, three years since he'd given up painting and moved to his private island. Well, he hadn't actually given up painting. It had given up on him. All those wonderful ideas that had come to him had suddenly dried up. He could only paint one thing over and over again. Thank God he had done so well before his dry spell—make that a drought—had come upon him. It all started with those damn dreams... He shook his head. He'd better clean the man up.

He went to the bathroom and returned with a washcloth to clean away as much of the sand and grit as he could. He wiped the man's face and chest. Then, as he began to move lower, the man stirred. He groaned slightly and turned over. And Lane was left to feast his eyes on one of the best asses he'd ever seen. Now, he was really in trouble. Thankfully, the man couldn't see how aroused he'd become. He quickly wiped the backside of the man off and retreated. He studied the man. They appeared to be around the same age. Lane had just turned thirty-five a month ago. How is this all going to play out? Well, tomorrow is another day. He smiled wryly. Thank you, Miss O' hara.

The man seemed to be resting peacefully, so he extinguished the candle, drew a sheet over the man's perfect body, and left to go check outside for any other shipwrecks. And to stop that damn banging door!

Another half-hour of searching turned up nothing, except more boat debris. He hadn't even found the main part of the boat. Perhaps it had sunk and would wash up later. The winds had started to subside somewhat and he thought that the worst was probably over—at least as far as the weather was concerned. His houseguest was another matter entirely.

He returned to the house and checked on the man—still safe and sound—then retired to his front room for, hopefully, a night of well-deserved rest. His bed certainly could have accommodated the two of them, but he didn't want the man to freak-out when he woke up and found himself in bed with another man. Besides, Lane would never have gotten a wink of sleep with that gorgeous body next to him. It was going to be hard enough sleeping in the next room. And he did mean hard. He closed his eyes and tried to envision something other than this god from the sea.

✳ ✳ ✳

Lane was scrambling a batch of eggs as he watched the wind still whipping the trees outside. The rain had subsided, but the wind was still raging strongly. He hadn't found any other bodies—thank God—and only more pieces of wood and sail, nothing substantial. It appeared that this Robinson Crusoe's Friday would be here for a while, at least until the next boat came with his stores. As he stirred and ruminated over his houseguest, he heard a noise and looked up.

*Crash!* Lane dropped the pan and it fell to the floor, scattering fluffy yellow yolk everywhere. Oh my God! It can't be.

"I'm sorry. Are you all right? I didn't mean to startle you," a male voice said.

Lane, flustered, scurried for paper towels and a sponge to clean up the mess. "I'm fine... I just... I mean, are you all right. You... you look fine," he sputtered. That was the understatement of the year. He looked perfect, Lane thought. If he'd been in an accident you couldn't tell. All the mess must have been just dirt and seaweed, because this man was perfection to the nth degree. And not only that, he was just wearing Lane's old white... white, for God's sake... nylon shorts. He might as well have not been wearing anything. It left nothing to the imagination. His anatomy was perfectly outlined. In fact, the man seemed more naked—and sexier—than he had last night. And that face!

The man grinned, revealing straight white teeth, and Lane thought he saw a glint off one of them. Those startling blue eyes... I'm doomed.

"I borrowed a pair of your shorts, as you can see. I hope you don't mind. I seem to have lost my clothes along the way."

"Uh, not at all. They've never looked better. I mean... take what you like." He bent down to clean up the eggs. Did I really just say that? What's that line about your inner voice? I certainly don't have one. "Are you hungry? I'm sure you must be after your ordeal."

"Famished. I can put on some other clothes if you like. I'm kind of used to not wearing much, being on the boat and by myself and all. Of course, I see you're not wearing much either."

Lane suddenly felt naked. "What you're wearing is fine. There's no one around but you and me." He glanced down between his bent knees at his own shorts, which had become abnormally tight. The reason was obvious. Now, how was he going to stand up? He couldn't clean the floor forever. Maybe the cooking island would be tall enough if he stood close to it. And crouched a little. He stood. Not too bad. Just a little awkward.

"A little problem there?" The man grinned again, eyes traveling to Lane's crotch.

Lane felt himself turning bright red. How had the man known? It looked as if the man's own shorts were getting a little fuller, if that were possible.

"Hey, it's only natural." Pearly whites flashed. "Want me to get some more eggs?"

Nonplussed. Yes, that was the word. I am nonplussed. "Sure. And some milk... and butter, too. Thanks."

Lane finished cleaning up.

"Here."

"Ah!" Lane jumped back and knocked into the man.

"Sorry. I didn't mean to startle you... again. Maybe I should leave you alone."

"No, no, it's all right. I was just woolgathering. I do that, being by myself." He took the eggs. "Just set the milk and butter there."

The man reached around Lane and set the items next to him. The man was a hairsbreadth behind him and Lane could feel the warmth radiating from him and smell a clean, yet musky scent coming from him. "My name's Adam," the man whispered in his ear.

The hairs on the back of Lane's neck stood up. He thought he might swoon. Instead, he replied, rather throatily, "Lane. I'm Lane."

Then, still with a whisper, "Nice to meet you... Lane." He put his hands on Lane's bare shoulders and leaned into him. "Thanks for saving my life."

Lane could feel the entire length of the man—no, not man, Adam—pressed up against his backside. "You're welcome," he managed to choke out.

"I like a lot of butter in my eggs." Adam grabbed the half-stick and tossed it into the pan. "Fluffy, not runny. And a lot of salt. Boy, am I bossy. Make them however you want. I'm sure they'll be great. I bet everything you do is great." He faced Lane now. "What do you do, Lane?"

Was Adam flirting with him? It sure seemed like it. Lane felt... nonplussed... again. Lane stared into those sea blue eyes. I'm drowning. "I paint. Or, at least I used to."

"Paint? Like houses?" Adam said in disbelief.

Lane grinned. "No. Like art. Although, sometimes I wish it were houses."

"Do you paint portraits or landscapes or seascapes? Wait! Lane... You're not Lane Tennant are you? Of course you are. I should have seen it right away. Your face was everywhere. The art world's hottest new face, in every respect. Your artwork is amazing. Then, what was it... three years ago? You just vanished. The great Lane Tennant mystery. Everyone tried to find out where you were. Were you kidnapped? Were you dead? Were you holed up with the Dalai Lama?"

"The Dalai Lama?" Lane interrupted.

"Yeah, there were all sorts of stories. Didn't you hear? Oh, I guess you didn't, because you were here. A little isolated. No TV or anything. You know you disappointed the art world, as well as the droves of adoring females, and a lot of males, who all wanted to jump your bones. Weren't you named People Magazine's 'Sexiest man of the year'?"

"Wow. I guess you know more things about me than I do."

"I read everything about you. I love your work. You're an incredible artist. You speak to my heart."

Lane looked into Adam's face—that amazing face—and believed every word. The honesty was blatant and refreshing. He had gotten so tired of the sycophantic kowtowing of the people that had surrounded him. As a matter of fact, if he hadn't hit his "dry spell" he would have left the art world anyway. He loved painting for what it was. An art. If people liked what he painted, fine. If not, fine too. Although, the money for the first several years had been nice. At least he hadn't had to worry where his next meal was coming from. And the money had allowed him to buy his little island and retire. But, he was forced to admit, solitude was wearing thin. And this man... Adam... he smiled inwardly—the First Man—had swept in like a breath of fresh air. A hurricane really. Well, he did come in with the storm. Maybe it was a sign. No. He knew it was a sign. Especially that face. How could it not be?

"Are you woolgathering again? Do people really use that word? I guess so, because now we've both used it in the space of twenty minutes. You need to put the eggs in the pan before the butter burns."

"Oh, right." Caught off guard. Nonplussed. Spellbound. Transfixed. Enamored. What Twilight Zone episode had he stepped into. Could things get any more bizarre?

"So why did you quit?

"I... I... "

"Was that rude? I'm sorry. I just say what I feel. Honesty is not always the best policy. Believe me. I've gotten into so much trouble just being honest. And slapped a few times, too. And punched out." He paused, then gripped Lane by the shoulders and faced him. "Please don't punch me out. You look really strong, and you're a couple of inches taller, and I was just in a shipwreck, and I'm injured." He held the sincerity for a long moment and then burst out laughing. "Sorry. I'm a really bad liar."

Lane couldn't help but laugh along with him. Then he sobered up and said in all seriousness, "You don't think I could punch you out?"

Adam's face dropped and he released Lane. "Would you?"

Now it was Lane's turn to grin. "After I saved your life? What kind of terrible host do you take me for?"

The warm smile returned to Adam's face. "I think you are the best host there ever was. And the hottest." He stepped back, faltering slightly, and gripped the counter. "I'm sorry. I shouldn't have said that."

"No, you shouldn't have." Lane stared into the oceanic eyes. "At least not till after breakfast." *He said I'm hot.*

"All right!" The blue pools twinkled again. "I love your hazel eyes, and can we have bacon, too?"

"Well, that was part of the menu." *He loves my eyes.*

"And toast? Juice? Bagels? Cream cheese? Oh, and cereal. If you have oatmeal it would be even better."

"I think so. Shipwrecking works up an appetite, I gather. How about some coffee to start?"

"That's a given. I think I'm going to like being a castaway for a while." He paused. "Um, how long is a while?"

Lane wasn't quite sure how to respond. Things were moving way too fast. He felt as if he were already in over his head. There were so many questions to ask. "There is a boat that comes every three weeks to deliver food and supplies." He poured out the coffee. "Other than that, I have a small motorboat, in case of an emergency, that would probably take you to the mainland." Lane felt a surge of melancholy at the thought of Adam leaving right away. Had he really missed human interaction that much? Or was it just interaction with this man, who was so open and ridiculously charming and handsome?

"Oh, that's all right. I'll wait for the supply boat." He looked up from pouring his coffee and stared at Lane. "If that's okay with you?"

Lane heard a little trepidation in Adam's voice. He smiled gently. "That's fine."

Adam let out a small sigh of relief. "I hope the boat just came yesterday."

Lane chuckled. "It did."

"Good." He winked at Lane. "That means that we'll have... " He paused and fixed his stare on Lane. "Lots of... f... " He paused again for effect, and slowly aspirated the f. "Food!"

Lane laughed with him. "Speaking of which I think most everything's ready. Let's eat."

There was a companionable silence between the two men while they ate, which gave Lane a chance to think about what was happening and what he was going to do about it. This man was extraordinary, in more ways than one. But what did that mean? The mutual attraction was obvious. But who was he? Where had he come from? Why now? Could he trust this man? He already had, he decided. But could he tell him everything? Could he tell him about his painting?

"What's another word for woolgathering?"

Lane started. "How about 'ruminating.'"

"Ruminating. Well, that's what you were doing again." Adam slapped his bare chest. "And here you've got this incredibly hot guy sitting across from you and all you want to do is gather wool? Are you into sheep?" He stared at Lane. "Baaaaaa! Baaaaaa! Are you excited yet? Do you think I'm hot? Maybe I should eat standing up. I know you like these shorts."

"You have no idea."

"Oh, I think I do."

"Are you always this... bold? We've just met."

"Uh huh."

"I guess that's why you get slapped and punched out."

"Uh huh."

"Have you had enough to eat? I think there might still be a steak or two I could fix."

"Maybe later. And I know we've just met, but I feel like I know you. Maybe it's because of your awesome paintings. They speak to me. I feel connected. Would you like to take a walk with me and show me your island? The wind's still blowing, but it's stopped raining, and maybe we can find some flotsam or jetsam from my boat—may she rest in peace. Or pieces, as the case may be."

"I'd like that." Paintings. That could definitely be the connection, Lane mused. "It's been a while since I've strolled the island, and I've never shown it to anyone."

"Really? I'm honored. I'm honored anyway just to be able to be with you."

Lane quirked his mouth. "You know, if I had heard that back in New York three years ago, I would've headed for the nearest exit. Thank you."

"For?"

"Being sincere."

"To a fault."

"Not yet."

"Just wait. I'm sure I'll come out with something inappropriate. And then you'll punch me out. It's okay, though. I'm kind'a used to it." Then Lane watched as Adam struggled with himself to say his next words. "Lane, whatever I tell you will always be the truth. I need you to believe that. All right?"

Lane stared at him, not sure if he was totally comprehending. Actually, he was sure he wasn't, but he sensed the magnitude of these words for Adam, how hard they were for him to utter, and the depth of importance of them. "Yes. I will believe whatever you tell me."

"Thank you. Do you believe in kismet, fate, destiny?"

"No, I think... " What did he think? He wasn't sure anymore. How could he deny what was right in front of him? Was it fate? It sure was something. Something extraordinary. Something... wonderful. "Yes, I think it's a possibility," he found himself saying.

"Like this? Like this strange connection that's happening between us?" Adam's eyes deepened. The bright blue became almost stormy.

Lane was sure his reaction was similar. He began to feel very warm again. "Yes. Like this."

"Good. Because I believe in it. Now, let's go for our trek across your beautiful island."

"Do you always move this fast?"

"When it's right. This is right. Besides, logistically, dating is a little difficult. Unless, you consider breakfast our first date. In fact, let's say it is. I like that. You took me to your place—carried me really, I guess—and made me breakfast. Although, usually, breakfast comes after the night before. Of course, you did get me into your bed. Alone, alas. I was alone, wasn't I? I didn't miss anything?"

Lane was outright laughing now. "You're amazing."

"No. I'm not amazing. Later. Then I'll be amazing." He put an arm affectionately around Lane's shoulder. "Let's go."

They walked companionably across the island for a while. Lane pointed out some of his favorite places to sit and watch sunsets and read. Then they chatted about art and some of Lane's better pieces. All the while the wind whipped about them. Lane found himself very happy to be talking and sharing all of this with Adam, that is until Adam asked, "Are you working on anything now?"

"Uh, not really."

"Hey, I told you that I was always honest. How come you're prevaricating with me?" Adam demanded.

Lane stopped walking. Decision-making time. "Let's sit over here out of the wind." He indicated a cluster of palm trees to his right. How do I tell him? He'll never believe me. Then again, maybe he will. Adam was, in a word: unique.

They sat side by side and Adam reached over and took Lane's hand. "It's all right. Don't worry. You can tell me."

And Lane somehow knew he could. That simple touch had unlocked something within him, something he had kept securely behind closed doors—literally and figuratively. "It started one night after my last big show in New York," he began. "It had gone very well. My agent was over the moon. He said it the most successful art show in thirty years. He thought that every piece I'd shown had sold that night. Then, he yelled out that everyone wanted a piece of the "Great Lane Tennant." And I realized he was right. Oh, not just a piece of my art, but a piece of me. That's when it hit me. I didn't want to do this anymore. I was no longer a person. I was like this object, this icon. And I hated it. It appeared that I had hundreds of friends, but not really. I went home alone. Well, not all the time, but practically speaking. I had sex, of course, I could have had it every night if I'd wanted... sorry. It sounds like I'm this big stud."

Adam squeezed his hand. "Actually, you are. But I know what you mean. Please go on."

Lane smiled slightly at Adam. "Thanks. But really all I wanted was one someone to go home with. I guess everybody does. But when you've got celebrity, nothing is real anymore, especially the people. I didn't know who was sincere and who was just out to get a piece of the "Lane pie." The more successful I got, the more reality slipped away. I was getting further and further away from my goal of finding someone to share my life with. I know it sounds cliché and pathetic, but I would have traded all my success for just someone to love and to love me back for who I am, and not this image of what I'd become. I knew I had to get away and sort out my life, and decide what I really wanted. That night the dreams started. Then, every night for a while, it was the same or a slight variation of the same dream. There would appear this—" Lane stopped.

"This?"

"This man who... " Lane couldn't say it.

"Let's go swimming." Adam dragged Lane to his feet.

"But the storm—"

"The storm's over and wind has died down enough. Don't you like to swim?"

"Yes, but—"

"Good. It's my passion. Well, one of them anyway." He winked at Lane. "Let's see if you can keep up." He raced to the shore, stripped off his shorts, and dove into a wave that was just breaking into shore.

Lane stood at the edge of the water and waited for Adam to pop up.

He waited.

And waited.

He was starting to become alarmed, when all of a sudden a sodden, blond head popped up out of waves about thirty yards out and yelled, "What are you waiting for? This is great! The water's just right. Take off your shorts and join me."

Lane hesitated a moment. Was he suddenly turning shy? He didn't have a problem with nudity. But he wanted to be perfect for Adam. Of course, he knew he wouldn't come up short in the dick department. Adam had already seen him aroused. It was... Oh hell. He was just being stupid. He doffed his shorts and dove in. He came up maybe twenty yards out from shore and looked around for Adam. But he'd disappeared again. The water was cool, but not too cold.

Lane felt a tug at his leg and for a moment thought Shark! Then a body slithered up his torso and met him face to face. "Did I scare you?"

"No."

Adam cocked an eyebrow.

"Maybe, for a second. There are sharks in these waters, you know. I've never seen one, but I'm sure they're here. I mean they're everywhere. It's the ocean and... "

A mouth closed down over his. Lane found himself transported. The kiss went on for minutes, and Lane lost himself in the sensational singularity of it. His body was caressed by hands and waves, both performing an erotic dance over him. His own hands also mixed with the water and the flesh of Adam, causing tingles and pulses everywhere he touched and was touched. "You're incredible," he heard in his ear.

And then Lane realized that there was no more water around them. They were standing on shore, still embracing and caressing.

How had they gotten back? He didn't remember swimming. They had been a ways out. Had the tide brought them in? He felt slightly awkward without the protection of the water around him. Although, the water certainly hadn't provided any sort of barrier from Adam's incredible body.

"This is the best swim I can ever remember having," Adam said as his nose nuzzled Lane's.

"Me too," was all Lane could manage.

"Shorts? Or no shorts?"

Lane just stared.

"To go back to the house, shorts probably," Adam decided. "Don't want to injure anything along the way. May need it for later."

Lane felt himself hardening more at the thought.

Adam pushed back slightly and looked down. "Definitely need it for later. Very nice, by the way."

Lane felt himself redden.

"And you blush, too. How adorable." Adam reached down and grabbed Lane's shorts, which conveniently lay next to them. "Here." He dropped Lane's shorts onto his erection. "That's cute. You could wear them like that. You could probably hold your whole wardrobe there." Adam grinned and scrambled to get his own shorts.

"You're too much," Lane said, laughing as he properly donned his shorts.

"I hope so... or at least enough." Adam wiggled his hips at Lane, erection flailing from side to side, before pulling on his own shorts.

Lane felt his jaw drop a little, then went to Adam and reached out and took his hand.

Adam smiled and squeezed. "Let's walk back to the house... slowly. I love the sensuous tension of anticipation."

"I'm dying," Lane groaned.

"Then, let's change the subject."

"All right, then. You haven't told me anything about yourself. That's all we've talked about is me. You must think I'm an egomaniac," Lane said on their stroll back to the house.

"Not too much of one." Adam grinned. "But I do think you're fascinating."

This took Lane off guard and he pulled up abruptly. "So tell me, what do you do? Why were you out in the storm? Where are you from? Are you single?" No, no, no, no, no! He'd done it again.

"I give day cruises from various islands. I was out sailing for my own enjoyment and thought I could beat the storm. I'm from different ports of call. And yes, I'm single." He raised his eyebrows quizzically at Lane. "Those questions are answered. What else?"

Lane analyzed the answers. "You could expound a little more. I just threw those questions out randomly. I didn't mean them as specific questions."

"Didn't you?" Adam grinned knowingly.

"Maybe a couple of them. I guess the single one. But I really do want to know about you because... " He paused. How far should he go with this? "Because I think I've met you before or... or... "

"Dreamed about me?"

Lane dropped his jaw and Adam's hand. "Yes. How did you know?"

"Lucky guess... E.S.P. Hope." Adam's eyes darkened and became intense.

"I have to show you something," Lane said, very serious now.

Adam grabbed both of Lane's hands. "It's okay. I'll believe you."

Lane forced a smile. "Let's go."

They didn't talk anymore until they reached the house. They went inside to the back of the house. "This is my studio." Lane indicated the closed door. He reached for the knob and thrust the door inward.

The room was all windows on three sides—an overwhelming effect. There were canvases everywhere: on easels, leaning against windows, and laying on the floor. None were portraits, but they all contained just one lone figure—the same figure, in varying poses and atmospheres. A man. Adam.

Adam stepped into the room and scanned. Lane found himself holding his breath.

"Well, I approve your subject matter," Adam finally announced.

"What?" This was the last thing Lane expected Adam to say. "But why? How? Who are you?" Lane was almost whining now.

"Apparently... your dream man." Adam quirked a slight smile.

"Yes, but how is this possible? I dream you. I paint you. Yet, we've never met. Whenever I pick up a brush, I try to paint something different, but it's always the same! Oh, the settings and backgrounds are different, but the subject is always the same. I can't seem to help myself. It's always you."

"I can't explain it... yet," Adam said as he walked around and studied the pictures.

"Yet? Yet? What do mean yet?'" Lane was becoming frantic... and a little scared. He grabbed Adam by the shoulders. "Tell me!"

"I can't. I don't have the answers. But I'll try to find out."

"Find out? How?"

"You'll just have to trust me." Adam stared directly into Lane's pleading eyes. "I'll be back. I promise." He pushed Lane's hands gently away, then turned and walked out the door.

Lane stood there, stunned. He stared around the studio at the multitude of Adams around him—all the different expressions and moods. He had seen living evidence of them over the past day: the humor, the delight, the playfulness, the desire, the passion. He had captured them all perfectly. This was his dream man.

This was the man he loved.

Yes, loved. He had to admit it. How could it be anything but love? He had known this man for years. He had slept with him night after night in his dreams. And now he had just let him walk right out of his life. He found it a little overwhelming. After all, he was still mind-boggled over it. And really, where could Adam go? It was a small island. Unless, he took the boat. Lane rushed to the door and headed out of the house and down the beach to where the motorboat was docked.

It was still there, bouncing in the slight waves that continued to buffet the shore. Lane let out an audible sigh of relief. What had Adam meant when he'd said, "yet?" That he couldn't explain it yet. What did Adam know that he wasn't telling him? He must find him. He needed answers. Had he scared him off? Who wouldn't be scared? Adam must think he was some kind of psycho-stalker. But they hadn't ever met. What was going on? Maybe he was crazy. He'd been alone on this island for over three years now. Maybe he was delusional. Maybe all of this was just in his mind. Maybe Adam wasn't even here. Maybe he was just a figment—an imaginary friend. He had to laugh for a moment. At least when he made up an imaginary companion, it was a perfect one.

"No," he said aloud. "You have to be real. No one could have made up that kiss. I'm going to find you and straighten this all out." Who was he talking to? Maybe he was crazy. He would find Adam anyway.

\* \* \*

After hours of searching, Lane returned to the house, making one last check to see if the boat was gone. He hadn't been able to find Adam anywhere. It was as if he'd disappeared. Like he'd never been there. It was getting dark and he was exhausted, physically, mentally, and emotionally. Mostly, emotionally. He'd called out Adam's name till he was hoarse. He was done in. Adam was gone—

or had never been. He'd manifested the man from the pictures he'd painted. He'd been that desperate, he'd decided. A dream man. That was it. He took off his shorts and lay down on the bed. His eyes closed and his brain shut down.

* * *

Lane felt the hands first. Then the smell. Musky. Salty. Sweaty. Like sea air. The hands caressed his shoulders and back, slowly sliding down his sides and stroking his buttocks. Kneading, squeezing. He groaned with pleasure. "Where were you?" he began.

"Later," was all Adam said.

The hands slid to Lane's front, and Adam turned Lane on his side, stroking and massaging his thighs, and stopping all conversation. The mouth began to work on his neck, the tongue sliding up to encompass his ear. The hands moved up to his inner thighs and groin, now lightly tickling and brushing the sensitive skin there. Lane totally succumbed to the amazing impressions those hands and fingers were creating, while the tongue and mouth drove him wild with desire. He was painfully hard, waiting for the hands to reach their goal. He was in heaven; he was in hell. The teasing was torturous and sublime. He could feel the fully aroused form pressed up against his back, slowly writhing and eking out every possible nuance of sensation. Each nerve on his backside and neck was firing at the same time. And just when the hands seemed ready to capture him, they gripped his hips and turned him around so that they were face to face. Their mouths unerringly captured one another. Lips, tongues, and teeth became the new sources of inspiration.

He'd come back. Adam. His dream man had come back. And now it was Lane's turn to explore him. While kisses blended into one another, Lane's hands made a journey over Adam's magnificent form. He didn't want to miss one square inch. He wanted to return the feelings and sensations Adam had just given him. And he did. Starting with Adam's incredible swimmer's shoulders and slowly working his way down, working and plying his fingers on Adam's shoulder blades and broad lateral muscles. Grabbing and tugging, and slowly cupping and pulling Adam's taut bottom into his own ever more powerful erection. But Lane wanted more.

He also wanted to taste every part of Adam, to taunt him to the brink of insanity. But Adam seemed to have his own agenda. "Let me go first," Adam said, and plummeted to Lane's neck and began to devour Lane as if he were his last meal. Then, just before Adam's mouth descended on Lane's chest, he said, ever so softly, "I told you I'd come back." And then one very erect nipple was covered with mouth and tongue.

Lane almost exploded right then. He had come back. This wasn't a dream. And even if it was, he'd rather have this dream than any reality he could come up with. Adam's mouth and tongue worked lower, nipping and pulling, and laving over every pore. Then, just as he did with his hands, Adam's mouth got perilously close to Lane's pulsing erection. Lane could feel the hot breath blowing on him there, and then, instead of taking him in, the open mouth covered his inner thigh just below his genitals. The deception was agony and ecstasy. Lane was so lost he couldn't tell one from the other. Could making love ever get better than this? Adam raised his head. "Ready?"

Lane's mind exploded. Every nerve now centered on one point. His hands clutched Adam's shoulders with a bestial vigor. Then came a blinding white flash of light.

Nirvana.

* * *

Many torrid, sweaty hours later, Lane lay with his head nestled in Adam's shoulder. Adam slowly brushed his hand back and forth over Lane's slightly stubbled jaw. Lane chuckled lightly.

"What's so amusing?" Adam said, still caressing the stubble.

Lane, whose hand had been resting between Adam's legs and was slowly fondling the soft skin of Adam's testicles, now gave a slight squeeze.

"Careful. I may need those for later," Adam moaned.

Lane continued the pressure. "I was just thinking that if this is afterglow, we ought to be able to light Manhattan for a week."

"Cute."

Another squeeze. Adam gasped. "Want to try for a month?"

"Hell. Why not go for a year."

Then Lane's mouth replaced his hand.

\* \* \*

Dawn was breaking, and the day promised to be perfect, with all signs of the storm gone. This time Adam was nestled under Lane's shoulder, one hand played with his chest. All was perfect. Lane hugged Adam hard. "I love you, Adam."

Silence. Then, "I know you do."

Lane's stomach clenched. He thought he might throw up. He thought he might cry. He tried not to think at all. This wasn't how it was supposed to go. What went wrong? What had he done? Maybe Adam was just afraid of the "L" word. Hell, did it really matter? He had him, that was enough. Wasn't it? He'd give him time. After all, he'd known Adam for over three years. Well, not physically, but in his dreams and paintings. He felt as if he knew him. But did he? Give him time.

"I have to go," Adam started to rise.

"Where? Do you want me to come along?" Lane hoped he didn't sound desperate.

"No. Maybe later."

He said, "Later." That's good. Isn't it? "Okay, fine. Do you want to eat first? I know I'm starving."

"No, you go ahead." He got up and went to the bathroom.

Lane went to the kitchen to make coffee. He shouted to the back of the house, "Do you want some coffee?"

Silence.

"Adam? Adam? Do you want coffee?" He went back into the bedroom, then checked the bathroom. The door was open. No Adam. "Now what?" He fell onto the bed and stared into space. The tears started to form. His heart breaking, his soul crushed.

\* \* \*

Sometime later, Lane found himself once again on the floor of his studio, staring at the face in the painting of the most wonderful person he'd ever known. What was he going to do? Where could he turn? And then a thought struck him. I need to paint. Right now. He got up, went over to the easel that held the last canvas of Adam he'd painted. Before removing it, he studied it. He'd gotten everything just right: the underlying humor in the eyes, the adventurousness, the raw sensuality, and the capacity for love. Then why didn't he say he loved me? He knew their lovemaking had been transcendent for both of them. Lane had felt it pouring from him with every kiss and touch. And he also knew that Adam had had a reason for responding with, "I know you do." Lane said this aloud. "What kind of bullshit answer is that?" It was almost condescending. He was starting to get angry. Maybe it would help brush the hurt away. "Ha!" How you could brush away the hurt when it went deep into your soul? Right now,

34

though, he needed to paint. He gathered his paints and brushes and began. Painting. That's what I need to do.

* * *

Several hours later, Lane stepped back to adjudicate his handiwork. He had become totally immersed in his painting, as he always did. It was finished. He tossed a cloth over the canvas.

"Hiding something?"

That voice. That rich sensuality. Adam.

"I'm not hiding anything." Lane let the implication hang in the air. He wanted to rush into Adam's arms, but he could sense that it wasn't the right thing to do.

A look of puzzlement crossed Adam's face. Then he gently smiled. "I missed you." He slowly walked towards Lane and opened his arms.

Lane let himself be enfolded, and fervently returned the embrace. "Me too." His voice cracked softly.

They basked in the moment, until Adam broke the spell. "I have to talk to you."

Lane could feel his entire being deflate. "I'm listening."

"Let's go in the other room. I need to sit and talk to you. This is too distracting." He gave Lane a squeeze.

Lane could fully feel the evidence of his distraction pressed against his own. "All right."

They went into Lane's den area. "How about a couple of brandies?" Adam gave that infectious quirk of smile at Lane. "I could use one. And I think you'll probably need it, too."

Lane cast him a wary glance. "Coming right up."

Lane returned with two healthily filled snifters and sat next to Adam on the sofa. "Here's sand in your eye," he joked, and touched his glass to Adam's.

Adam took a long sip. "Remember what I told you when we first met? Yesterday. Was it really only yesterday?" he said, more to himself than to Lane.

"Yes. To believe you."

"Right. Well, here goes." He breathed in deeply and took a large gulp from the snifter. "I'm from the sea—a Mer-man, to give it a name." Adam waited for a reaction. Lane stared at him, giving no discernable reaction, so he continued. "I was born in the ocean and grew up there. Evolutionists had part of it right when they said that all life came from the sea. Man did come from there. And they are still coming from there. Those of my race who are born in the sea have the ability to adapt to land if they so choose. Our adaptability has advanced over the years, and anatomically we adjust very quickly—gills becoming lungs etc., but no fish tails. That's pure fiction. Fish tales, if you will." He chuckled a little awkwardly at the pun and took quaffed some more brandy. "Yeah, well, biologically speaking I can't really explain it; I just know that it happens. And it also happens in reverse when we return to the sea. Lungs become gills. Hence, my little disappearing acts. I needed to go see my people for information... and advice." He looked down at his glass and laughed. "Maybe you should refill our glasses. I seem to have emptied mine. And I think you should finish yours off before I go on."

Silently, Lane finished his snifter, took the glasses, and went to refill them.

He returned and sat down. His demeanor unchanged.

"Thank you."

Lane nodded.

Adam took a gulp. "This is the kind of cool part. When my people stay in the ocean we age differently, much slower than here on the surface. And even if we stay for a while, our age progression is much slower. Maybe it's the water keeping us hydrated. It's probably why health gurus are always saying drink eight glasses of water a day. Drink plenty of liquids." He laughed again. And drank. "I wonder if brandy counts? Anyway, I know it's helping me tell you."

Lane gave his first reaction and slightly smiled.

Adam returned an uncomfortable grin. "Most of our people venture to the surface at some point. Some last a few days, some... years, like me... and some even longer. You see, after about twenty-five to thirty years, something happens within us, maybe it's the lack of total hydration, but we start to age as you do. Oh, we don't all of sudden become old crones and get all wrinkly, we just start to age naturally from where we are at that point in our life." He raised a hand. "And before you ask, I've been here twenty-three years. So, I'm a lot older than you are—in your years, anyway."

"Now, I don't kiss and tell, but I will tell you that I certainly haven't been a saint for the past twenty-three years I've been here. But I have never really let myself get involved—nothing serious. It's always just been for fun. And I never really found anybody worth my prolonged attention. Until now." He looked directly into Lane's eyes.

Lane returned the stare. He was so confused. But wanted Adam to continue. He drank from the glass and nodded.

"When I said 'sometimes,' some of our people stay longer, I meant... permanently. This is kind of the mystical part. If a man or woman finds a mate who they want to share their life with, then they give up their... Mer-existence and can never return to the sea. All contact is broken and their memories of that life gradually fade away. We don't know why. We think it has something to do with the magic power of love." He drank again. "But magic or no, the outcome is real. This is why I needed to go see my people. There has never been a gay Mer-man or Mer-woman who has fallen for someone on the surface. He cocked his head at Lane. "Are you getting all this?"

Lane nodded. "Go on."

"So, as I said, there have been straight Mer-men and Mer-women who have opted to stay, and they have never returned to the sea. But I figured I had it made since I was gay. I thought the whole lose-your-memory thing had to do with straight people and the procreation side of things. But, as I found out, it all has to do with the love side of things. So, I told them I had found someone. Someone special. But I needed to know that if I gave my heart, would I forever be banned from the sea. Are you still with me?"

Lane nodded.

"Now, about the dreams and the paintings," Adam continued. "I asked them what could have caused you to paint all those pictures of me without ever having known me. They discussed it—they being the elder members of my people—and discovered that the longer one remains on the surface the more chance that his or her life force, soul, essence would have a chance of being discovered or sensed. It seems that in my people our essences are stronger than those of people on land, and when we surface our essence becomes more vulnerable for someone on land to latch on to. But only if that someone is the one and only right person for them. The cool part, again, being that if this does happen, you know you've found your true mate. You picked up my essence and transferred it into your dreams and into your paintings. I don't know how it has worked with others. I only know that's how it worked for you. All of which, of course, didn't answer my other question of: Would I also lose my memory and not be able to return to the sea? The elders reasoned that it would probably follow suit for anyone who gave their heart, but as it had never happened before with a gay Mer-man, they couldn't say for certain. Big help, huh?"

Lane could still only nod, understanding dawning, while he clung to a shred of hope as to where this was all leading.

"So that is my dilemma. Profess my love and give up my sea life—under it anyway—or sail away and continue my carefree, if slightly empty, existence." He stopped.

"And now what?" Lane finally said.

"Now, the ball is in your court."

"Mine?" Lane said, totally mystified.

"Of course. Hey, don't you have any questions?"

"Only one."

"Which is?"

"Are you in love with me?"

Adam was totally taken aback. "That's it? That's the only question? You believe all that crap I just threw at you? Mer-people? What, are you nuts?"

"No. I'm in love with a man who told me I should believe him no matter what he said. And I do."

Tears sprang to Adam's eyes. He shook his head in disbelief. "How? How is it possible that I could find someone like you?" He stared lovingly at Lane. "You're the dream come true."

"Personally," Lane said, "I think I like being awake better... as long as I'm with you. Are you sure can you give up your other life?"

"We all move on. And hopefully move on to where we're supposed to be. I gave up my life under the sea years ago. That's why I seldom go back. My future wasn't there. This is a no-brainer. Not only do we have all the mystical signs pointing the way for us, we also have this." He pulled Lane to him and kissed him passionately.

The magic was instantly there. They both knew it, and always would.

"That's all I need," Lane said, breathlessly. "You're all I'll ever need."

"Ditto."

"Can I ask you something else now?" Lane said.

"Anything."

"Is that why you wouldn't say 'I love you' to me? Were you afraid of what would happen?"

"No. Yes. I was unsure. Not of my feelings. But of what all this might mean to you. How you would deal with it? Could you deal with it? I'd never told anyone before, and I knew if I committed to you that that would be it. You needed to know what you were getting into because there would be no going back. I would never give you up. I would pursue you until I died. My heart would give me no choice. Because if I didn't have you, I would have no life."

Lane took Adam's face lovingly into his hands. "I realize now that it was too late the night I painted my first picture of you. You became a part of me, a part that has been growing inside me ever since. And a part that has continued to grow, more so now that I've finally found you. You're the missing part of me that's made me complete."

The tears of happiness had been pouring down Adam's face since Lane had begun his confession. He embraced Lane with all the love that was inside him.

Lane kissed Adam's ear and whispered, "One more question. When you do say 'I love you,' is there going to be a big clap of thunder or something?"

Adam brushed the tears from his cheeks and looked into his love's sparkling eyes. "Let's find out." He grasped Lane's hands. "Lane Tennant, I love you."

They both lifted their heads to listen.

The calm skies let roar a clap of thunder that was surely heard to the oceans' depths.

Adam gave a huge grin. "I think that would be a yes." They embraced again. "Now, I want to go see your latest masterpiece. I think I might now have the right perspective to give it a proper evaluation." They linked hands and set off for the studio.

"It's absolutely perfect." Adam avowed as he stared at Lane's latest painting. "And my new favorite. I knew there was something missing from all these other pieces. Now, you've found it."

They both stared at the painting. There were two men standing in the foreground with an almost supernaturally beautiful sunset behind them. The bodies were joined, their gazes locked on one another. The unabashed love, obvious.

Lane turned into Adam and held him, gazing into Adam's watery blue eyes that mirrored the painting before them. "Yes, I have."

# PISCES

Pisces—The Fishes


Traits: Creative (especially in the arts), imaginative, sensitive, compassionate, kind, intuitive, sympathetic, malleable nature, receptive to new ideas, loves mysteries in all its guises.

"And the nominees for best actor in a leading role are: Harrison Ford—The Astronaut's Wife, William Macy—Death of a Salesman, Paul Walker—Lighter Than Air, Mark Wahlberg—Just One More Time, and Lake Hartwood—Intensity."

Lake sat waiting anxiously while Julia Roberts ripped open the envelope, knowing the television cameras were monitoring his every movement. He tried to keep a calm demeanor. This was the moment. He had worked hard his whole life, and it all came down to this moment in time. This award would certainly mean a lot to his career. His role in "Intensity" was every actor's dream. And if he won the Oscar, he would have his pick of roles. He was only thirty— well, thirty-four actually—but all actors dropped a few years from their age, and he could still play early twenties. With his blond hair, boyish good looks, and the fact that he worked out to keep in shape, nearly every day, he hoped to have a very long career. Yes, he had won the Golden Globe, but that didn't mean much really. It was all about the Oscar. He had coveted one since he was a teenager, when he decided he wanted to be an actor.

The audience laughed. What had Julia just said? Just read the damn card! Please! I'll show you, Dad. I'll show you who the queer loser is. Your son is a big star and an Academy Award winner. Got that? Winner! You're the loser, Dad. You!

"And the winner is..." Julia paused for effect. Her eyes met Lake's.

"Lake Hartwood for "Intensity!"

Lake was stunned. Had she just said his name out loud? No. They'd just made eye contact. He felt a nudge at his side.

"Go on, Lake. You won!" Drew Barrymore, his co-star shouted.

He rose and walked to the stage. He didn't hear the thunderous applause or feel anything. He was numb. His eyes focused on the statuette that Julia Roberts held out for him. He got to the microphone. She embraced him and thrust the statuette into his hands. She stepped to the side and nodded to him.

The audience quieted and waited for him to speak.

He had a speech prepared, but couldn't remember one word. He couldn't remember his name. Then his eyes met Drew's. She was openly crying. She had been his rock throughout the torturous shooting of the film. She had pulled him through the horrendous moments and the seemingly impossible scenes, when he had said he just couldn't do it. He had sat with her in his trailer. He'd cried with frustration and exhaustion while she had held his hand and encouraged him. He had played a dual role: twin brothers. One straight, one gay, and one of them a sociopathic killer, the audience not knowing who was who until the excruciatingly horrible, final scene. A scene that set Lake back several boxes of Kleenex and multiple sessions with Drew. She had become his confidante and best friend.

And now as he looked into her eyes, he felt her love pouring into him, and he began to speak, very slowly and softly. There was dead silence.

"I dreamed of this moment my whole life. I have worked and given everything to make something of myself, and to prove that, at least to me, I was a success. I've never had a successful relationship or had very many friends. I guess it's because I didn't think enough of myself, so how could I be good for anyone else. I, of course, am grateful to the Academy and everyone who worked on "Intensity." But I especially want to thank my co-star, Drew, who got me through some very difficult times during the filming."

He smiled at her. Her face streamed tears. He started to choke up; tears formed in his own eyes. "I know—" he swallowed. A tear broke free and trickled down his face. "I know that this is probably inappropriate, I mean, here, in front of you all, but this award, really, is for me." He looked at the statuette. "It not only validates me as an actor, but also as a person. It—" He swallowed hard again and another tear fell. "It makes me feel that... maybe, I'm worth something after all. Thank you."

Julia pulled him close. Her tears fell openly as well. Lake buried his face in her shoulder and she led him offstage.

The audience, which had been eerily silent, burst into spontaneous and uproarious applause. Many stood as Lake was escorted from the stage.

Lake attended the Governor's Ball that night, as well as Sir Elton John's soiree, and several other parties. His fellow actors were ebullient over his acceptance speech. And many actors who had never given him the time of day before were now his best friends. Lake was now the flavor-of-the-month. Or at least the night. And, of course, being the most photographed and interviewed winner of the night did not hurt his cachet either. The sycophants swarmed. What actor didn't want to have his picture taken? Especially, with the night's hottest actor. But in spite of all the lauds and good wishes, he still felt empty. It seemed an empty victory. He really had no one to share this with. There was Drew, of course. She was happy for him and loved him. But as a friend, not a lover. Lake had no one to go home to, except his dog. And he certainly had no family that cared. Personal victory would have to be his solace.

He'd left Elton's party early, about 3:00 A.M., and now he opened the door to his Sherman Oaks home. His dog waited anxiously at the entrance.

"Well, Sebaka... we won." The dog jumped up and put his paws atop Lake's 5' 10" frame. With one hand Lake rubbed one side of the Russian wolfhound; his other hand clutched his Oscar, and the dog gave him a hearty lap in the face.

"Unconditional love. You are man's best friend, Sebaka. Here, let me put Oscar down, so Daddy can show you how much he missed you.

The dog jumped down and ran down the hall to the bedroom to await Daddy's attention.

Lake went to the kitchen to fix to Sebaka's dinner. Or early breakfast. Then with dog food in one hand and Oscar in the other, he proceeded down the hall to his bedroom and his furry bed partner.

\* \* \*

The next morning, Lake received a wakeup call from Gerald Knight, the director of Lake's next film.

"Lake, honey, you absolutely have to be here tonight," the director oozed. "The producers are getting anxious and they want to know that you are one hundred and eight percent into this project. They need to hear from your oh so luscious lips that you're willing to do anything for them."

Lake wriggled in his skin. "First of all, Gerald, thank you so much for the Oscar congratulations."

"Oh yes, of course, darling. It will be great publicity for the film."

"And second, I told you we still need to discuss a couple of scenes before we begin shooting. I do have script approval on this, you remember."

"Yes, sweetie, I know. But the gang rape scene is crucial. We need to show what this guy has to go through. The harsh reality of it. It's got to look real. Remember your idol—mine, too—Christian Bale. He immerses himself in every project. Remember all that weight he lost for that "Machinist" movie? And that other one... Oh, you know. The one that didn't make any money. Thank God, the boy started eating again. He looked just dreadful. Now, I'm not asking you to do anything that Christian, I'm sure, wouldn't do. You do know he expressed great interest in this project. This role was made for you. And now with your Oscar hype, everyone, straight and gay, will be dying to see your next feature, especially since it features your incredibly hot body so well. The world will want to see Lake Hartwood bare his soul and everything else. I've even heard there are several betting pools online about the size of your penis. How big is it, anyway? I could use the extra cash."

"Big. Gerald, this is what I'm talking about." Sebaka nuzzled Lake's arm. Breakfast time.

Lake stroked the dog and continued, "I don't know if this would be so good for my image. Audiences see me as the strong, hero type. There's no redemption for the character. He's a victim."

"But, Lake, that's reality. We're trying to show that things always don't turn out for—

"I understand what you're going for. "Intensity" was a stretch. I took a chance and it paid off. Big time. But at least one of my characters was a good guy."

"Lake, I have to be honest. These guys won't do the film if you're not in it. No deal. I can't afford to... Let's just talk tonight, as a favor to me. I promise I'll defend you to the hilt. I'm sure we can work this out. You're a great actor. You can do anything. You're better than Christian. And better looking. He's never even been nominated. Has he? It doesn't matter. You're the best! See you tonight."

The phone went dead. If Gerald had sucked up any more to him, he would've been swallowed.

Lake flopped back onto his pillow. "Sebaka, I'm exhausted. That queen can talk a blue streak. I never should have committed to this film. I should have at least waited until after the Awards. You know script approval doesn't mean shit."

The dog stared at Lake and moved in for a lick.

"If I just walk out on this film, my rep's gonna stink. I'm not a big enough star yet that my career can handle that. Oscar or no Oscar. Why can't I just find some wonderful guy to take me away from this all? I hate the business of Show Business. People suck. I just want to be happy. And loved. And love someone."

He received another lick.

Lake hugged Sebaka tightly. "Yes, I love you. I'll always love you. Now, I'd better get ready and go face the dreaded Harry Malick agent. When I tell him I'm thinking of dropping out of the film, he's gonna shit a brick."

\* \* \*

Harry Malick, mid-size agent with big-time ego, sat looking stern as Lake entered his office. Lake guessed that Gerald might have pre-empted his appointment.

"Whadda ya mean ya don't wanna do the rape scene? And what's this script approval shit?" The Brooklyn in Harry came to the fore. "Baby, have I eva' steered ya wrong? Ya won a friggin' Oscar for that movie you was scared ta do." He wiped his greasy brow. "This one'll get ya another one. Guara-fuckin'-teed. The whole town's talkin' about it and ya haven't even started it yet. Babe, whadda ya doin' here, huh?"

Baby. Babe. Honey. These words could start to grate on you real fast. He knew this confrontation wasn't going to be pretty. Perhaps, he was wrong. No. It wasn't the rape scene or being nude. It was something else. It just didn't feel right. Everyone involved seemed to be desperate about the project. Why? He had yet to see the full script. He was told there were some "surprise" scenes that needed to be kept under wraps. From him? He was the star. Maybe, he thought sardonically, if he was real lucky, there'd be an orgy with a herd of sheep! Top secret? This wasn't Brian DePalma or M. Night Shyamalan. He wished. But with stars like Tom Cruise, Russell Crowe, and Mel Gibson getting bad press, he would be glad to fill some of their roles. He did have an Oscar after all.

He had totally tuned out Harry's rantings.

"So, Babe, whadda ya say? Ya gonna listen to Papa Harry?"

"All right, Harry. I'll go to Gerald's tonight and hear what he's got to say."

"That's my baby."

Grrr.

* * *

Lake was on his third Belvedere dirty martini in an hour and he was feeling no pain. But it didn't dull the gnawing feeling that he was about to make the worst decision of his life—even worse than telling his father he was gay.

Gerald had been schmoozing and chatting up the producers for the past hour. Priming them for the kill? He motioned Lake to join them.

This was it. Why was he hesitating? If things got really out of hand on the shoot, then he could walk. No. This picture had gotten too much press already. And it wasn't true that any publicity was good publicity. He could become Adrien Brody. He'd gotten an Oscar when nobody knew him and he's still struggling for roles. And he's a nice guy. Sure, guys like Cruise and Crowe and Gibson could take the bad P.R. They were superstars. People like bad boys. But Lake was Mr. All-American. Not quite a star, but in that nether region between superstardom and oblivion.

Adrien Brody. Oblivion. He took a step toward Gerald.

"Don't do it, Lake."

Lake stopped and turned around.

"Holy shit!" Lake prayed that wasn't out loud. The voice of admonition belonged to the most beautiful man Lake had ever seen: six feet tall, broad shouldered, tapered waist, almost pitch-black hair, and startling gray eyes placed in the perfectly square-jawed face of a god.

And then the god smiled.

A perfect smile.

Lake realized he had spoken out loud.

"I have never had that reaction before."

Lake heard a slight accent, possibly Russian, come from the god. He tried to compose himself. "I'm sorry. Were you speaking to me?"

"Yes. I said, don't do it."

"Don't do what?"

"Don't do what your heart tells you not to do."

Lake tried to decipher the statement. "I have to."

"Why?"

God, his eyes are so intense. Lake was hypnotized. "I... I... because everyone tells me I should." Jeez, that sounded lame.

"Oh."

Lake jerked his head back. "How do you know what I'm going to do?"

"I've been watching you for the past hour, through three Belvedere martinis I believe, and much... thinking, fidgeting."

Lake had never heard a word sound so sexy. He stared at the man, taking in the form-fitting, dove-gray polo shirt that accentuated the startling eyes and the deeper gray chinos that hugged the man in all the right places. Very nice.

"Lake, come on. They're waiting." Gerald stood to his right, a look of irritation on his face.

"I'll be right there, Gerald. I need to use the bathroom."

Gerald huffed. "All right. But hurry up. They're all primed for you."

They're primed? Then why did he feel like the fatted calf going to slaughter? He turned to the gray-eyed man. But he had disappeared.

Lake stared into the mirror of the over-sumptuously done gold and white bathroom. "What should I do?"

"Whatever your heart tells you."

The god was standing next to him. Where? How? This room was mostly mirrors. "How... "

"The door was unlocked."

"No, I... It doesn't matter. I have to go."

"Why?" The gray eyes looked almost sad.

"They're waiting for me."

"Why?"

"They... I... Because... I don't know how to say no. I'm afraid I'll make the wrong choice."

"What does your heart tell you?"

"To walk away."

"Then do it. Any decision made from the heart can never be wrong."

Lake stared. And believed him. "Who are you?"

"Yuri. Yuri Trofimov."

"You're Russian?"

"That was rhetorical, was it not?" His mouth quirked up to the right as he raised one eyebrow.

Lake felt himself flush. Even a partial smile was devastating. "Are you gay?"

The quirk turned into a full on, teeth blinding smile. Lake almost wanted to take a step back from the force of it.

"I assume that was rhetorical, also?"

Lake tried to regain some composure. "Oh God. I am so sorry. That was just plain rude. I never ask anyone that. Please forgive me."

"It is all right. I find you ochen privlekatyelny, also."

"What?"

"Very Attractive."

Lake stared into Yuri's magnetic eyes. He could feel himself being pulled forward, drawn into the depths of them. Two arms encircled his back, and just before lips met lips, the Russian murmured, "The door is locked." And then their mouths joined.

Lake had never, never, been kissed like this. He could feel the sensation in the tips of his fingers and toes. Incredible couldn't even begin to describe it. He felt as if the kiss touched his soul. Maybe it did. Who is this man? At the moment, Lake didn't care. He just wanted to stay locked in Yuri's arms forever. Nothing had ever felt so safe, secure, or right. This marvelous stranger had made him feel as if he'd come home at last.

A harsh rap on the door broke the magic moment.

"I didn't mean to do that, Lake. I don't why I did. I couldn't stop myself." Yuri stared into Lake's eyes. "Yes, I do. You are irresistible and a very special man. I need to go now. Follow your heart, dorogoy."

Lake nodded. "I'll be right out, Gerald." He turned to flush the toilet. When he turned back, Yuri was gone.

\* \* \*

"Thank you, gentlemen, and good luck with your film." Lake closed the door and walked out of the room. He heard Gerald say something about, "... never working in this town again." Somehow, Lake didn't believe it. He felt better about himself than he had in a long time. He'd just won an Oscar. He'd just said no to some very powerful, Hollywood types. And he'd just met the most incredible man and had the hottest kiss of his life. Life was good. His life was good. He never thought he would be able to say it. But at last he really felt it. "My life is good!" he shouted to the stars as he exited the Mulholland Drive mansion.

"And why would it not be?" came a voice from the darkness.

Lake turned to see Him standing there. "Where did you go?" he said, after recovering from the shock and joy of seeing Yuri before him.

"I thought it would be best to disappear." Yuri cocked his head to the side. "Your meeting went well?"

"Yes. I might have burned a couple of bridges, but what actor in Hollywood doesn't? Would you like to come to my house for a drink?" he blurted out, then sucked in a breath. Lake had never asked a guy he had just met back to his place. *What's wrong with me?*

"I do not think that would be a good idea, Lake. I need to—"

"Of course, you're busy. Who isn't?" Lake rushed on. "I didn't mean it to come out like it did. I... just wanted to talk... get to know you. I never ask guys back to my place. I'm not into the meet 'em, fu... " He caught himself as Yuri arched an eyebrow, then he continued, "Sleep with 'em and leave 'em thing. That's not me. Really. It's not. But you just seem different than other L.A. guys. Well, of course, you're Russian. That could be it. No. It's something else. It—" Lake stopped his babbling. Yuri was actually laughing at him. Even his laughter was sexy.

"Lake, you don't have to apologize or explain to me anything. I know you. You are a good man." Yuri hesitated, fumbling for speech. "I shouldn't... can't get involved."

Lake was crushed. "You've got a boyfriend."

"No. I don't."

"Are you sick?"

"No. I am well. It is complicated."

"Are you married? I thought we shared something special when you kissed me in there."

Yuri nodded slowly. "Yes, our kiss was very special. I think the word is unique. No, I am not married. But I have to be careful."

"I understand," Lake said, not understanding at all. "Could we take it slow? A movie? Dinner? Coffee?" He hoped he didn't sound desperate. "Please?" God! Now that was desperate.

"We will see. I cannot explain to you now."

Lake realized he had been holding his breath in anticipation of Yuri's response.

"We will see each other again. That is all I can promise. Will you accept that?"

Lake finally exhaled. He would have accepted a pat on the head from this man. "Yes. Yes, I will. I think we need to give this a chance at least."

"We will see, golubchik," the Russian reiterated, a worried look crossed his face. "Now, I must go. And your dog needs you."

"Right." Lake gave a half-smile and turned to look for the valet attendant. "How did you know I had a d—" But Yuri had vanished.

* * *

"Sebaka, I feel like I finally have control of my life," Lake said as he gently stroked the flank of his dog later in bed that night. "I know I did the right thing by turning down that rotten movie. And did I tell you? I've met the most incredible guy. No?" The dog pawed at Lake to let him know he'd stopped petting him. "I know you'd like him. He's Russian, just like you." Sebaka let escape a growl that came out like a purr. "You even have the same deep voice. Although, his is sexier." Another growl. "I'm pretty sure he's interested. He kissed me. And let me tell you... " He raised the dog's face to his. "If that's all I ever get from him is that kiss, I'll remember it forever. Whew!

That kiss was better than most of the sex I've had." Sebaka licked his face. "Nice try. Your kisses are good, too." He received another lap and then the two settled in for the night.

\* \* \*

The next morning, while sipping cappuccino at his favorite morning hangout, The Abbey, in West Hollywood, Lake scanned The Hollywood Reporter, just to see if word had gotten out yet about his exit from—what he called—"The Gang Rape Movie." The film had gone through several title changes and the current moniker was "Purgatory." How apt. Lake smiled, for he was no longer in his own purgatory. He was on the road to healing. He tossed aside the Reporter, finished off his capp, and left a couple of dollars on the table. He had an appointment with Harry at ten and didn't want to be late. He knew Harry would already be seething over his last night's decision.

He stepped off the curb to cross Santa Monica Boulevard and didn't see the car that came barreling down the street and was obviously not going to stop as Lake entered the crosswalk.

A tremendous jolt threw Lake backwards out of the crosswalk and back onto the sidewalk. He was stunned and the breath was knocked out of him. A horn blared in anger. He opened his eyes and looked up into two magnificent gray orbs. "Yuri," he gasped.

"You almost got yourself killed, dorogoy."

Lake couldn't help himself. He pulled Yuri's mouth to his in a searing kiss.

A few moments later, he heard applause. A crowd had gathered around the two after the almost accident. There were murmurs of, "That's Lake Hartwood. Who's the other hunk?" etc. While Lake had not publicly come out, he didn't hide his homosexuality either. This was the first time he'd kissed another man in public, on the mouth anyway. And certainly not in broad daylight. Let alone, while lying down on the sidewalk in the middle of West Hollywood! He just hoped there were no cameras. Well, too late now.

"I guess that means you are all right," Yuri dryly quipped.

"Yes." Lake stared hard into Yuri's eyes. "Who are you?"

"An angel."

"I'll say."

"I think we should get up before more of a crowd gathers." Yuri rose and helped Lake to his feet.

Lake brushed himself off and noticed a new tear in his jeans. Oh well. They were supposed to be ripped anyway. Yuri looked immaculate in a white tank top and khakis. Why isn't he dirty? He looks perfect. Lake turned to the small crowd. "I'm all right. Thank you all for your concern. My guardian angel just saved me."

A few people laughed and the crowd began to disperse.

"You believe me?" came the deep, accented voice.

"About what? You being an angel?"

Yuri nodded.

"Well, it would make sense. I mean, you pop up and disappear at will. And you did save me... twice. You certainly look like an angel. Only problem is... I don't believe in angels, and I'm sure that even if I did, I never heard of one with a Russian accent."

"We come in all nationalities." Yuri's look was serious and he seemed almost hurt.

"You're serious."

"Da, dorogoy."

Lake began walking, shaking his head. "I knew it. I knew you were too good to be true. I'm late for my appointment. Maybe I'll see you later—no, no, I can't. I can't see you." He stopped, but Yuri had vanished.

✳ ✳ ✳

The rest of Lake's day went by in a haze. Curiously, Harry hadn't upbraided him for walking off "Purgatory." He'd actually seemed somewhat relieved. And he hadn't heard from Gerald or any of the producers. They were probably too busy scrambling around for his replacement. He intended to dive into a couple of scripts he had at home that looked promising, provided he could clear his mind of the devastating Yuri. The Angel. He'd been haunted by thoughts of the handsome Russian all day long. How could he be an angel? Yes, he did seem to appear and disappear at will, and he showed up when Lake needed him. But... he'd kissed him. That didn't seem very angel-like. A gay angel? A Russian gay angel? That kiss was certainly heavenly though.

At home Lake continued his diatribe with Sebaka, who always listened. "For the first time in my life I feel like I'm in control. I know it's more than just winning the Oscar, although that helped. Harry treated me like a human for once. I had a great workout at the gym, except for the few twinges where Yuri'd knocked me to the ground. I escaped being hit by a car—thanks to Yuri, again, and I kissed an angel. Again.

He brushed the dog's long coat. "Could he really be an angel?"

"Sebaka is Russian for dog, you know," a deep voice said from behind the couch where Lake was sitting.

Lake jumped up. Sebaka just moved over and stared at the Russian. "How did you get in here? Sebaka, why didn't you bark?" The dog kept staring.

"Animals—especially dogs—like angels. They can sense goodness." Yuri smiled.

But... but you can't be an angel. It's impossible!"

"No, it's not," Yuri simply stated.

"Why?" Lake said weakly.

"Because I'm here."

"But you kissed me." Lake hadn't meant to say it. But it had slipped out. Probably, because he couldn't forget it.

"I know. Sometimes things happen. Angels are not God. We still have many human traits. Attractions are possible but not encouraged. It can get very complicated."

Lake felt hypnotized. Was it possible? Yuri seemed so matter-of-fact. He'd try another tactic. "Why are you here?"

"To help guide you."

"Why?"

"You are a very special and good man."

"No, I'm not."

"You are. You just need to realize it. I believe you have already started."

Lake couldn't deny it. "I want to be good. I want to be... something."

"You are something. Do not let your past destroy your future."

"Would you like a drink?" Lake wasn't ready to deal with his past. "I mean, do angels drink?"

A chuckle. "Da."

"I can't believe I'm starting to believe you. It's either true or you're the most original stalker ever. What would you like? Oh, vodka, I presume?"

"Straight. Do you have any pickles?"

"Pickles? I think so."

"It is the real Russian way of drinking."

"Sit down and make yourself at home. I'll be right back." An odd smile came to his face as he left the room.

When he came back, Yuri was seated on the couch brushing Sebaka gently. "Pickles. Shot glasses. Vodka." He poured, "Nas drovya," and raised his glass to Yuri's.

Yuri smiled. "You do know that this is not the way we drink in Russia. We do not even have these little glasses."

Lake was already doubtful of these size glasses. He drank, but he usually stayed away from shots. "Unless you want me totally drunk, very fast, this will have to do. Now what do we do the pickles?"

"Eat it. After you drink the vodka."

"Like lime after tequila? Okay. Here goes."

They tossed back their shots. Lake grimaced as he bit into the pickle. "Whoa! That's strong." He paused. "Hey, this is pretty good. I like the pickle part. It really complements the vodka."

"Da. Would you like another?" Yuri started to pour.

"I don't know. I... " He stared into Yuri's intense eyes. Was he seeing more than he thought? Or had the vodka already taken over. In any event... "Just one more," came out of his mouth.

Yuri smiled again and poured. "A tuy. To you."

Lake felt himself blush. "Thank you," he said softly, and stared intently into Yuri's eyes as he drank. This time he didn't notice the fierce assault on his throat as he swallowed. He brought the pickle to his mouth, his eyes still locked with Yuri's as they both bit together.

The air was now thick with testosterone. Yuri ran his tongue over his lips cleaning away the remaining brine-vodka mixture from them. Lake's throat went dry as he watched Yuri.

"Dorogoy, I have to do this." He ran his tongue over Lake's lips, slowly, savoring the combination of tastes there.

Lake closed his eyes and gave in to the exquisite sensations coursing through him. His lips tingled, burned, buzzed. They parted, and he felt Yuri's tongue enter his mouth. Their tongues entwined in an erotic tango. Lake felt Yuri's arms automatically enfold him and his responded in kind. Their terpsichore of tongues continued as they lay back on the couch.

Yuri's tongue now trailed down Lake's neck as he pushed Lake's T-shirt off and up over his body.

Then flesh met flesh. Somehow Yuri had managed to remove his own shirt, and their two muscular chests met and seared one another.

Lake openly gasped when he felt Yuri's nipples meet his own. His hands roamed Yuri's well-formed back; Yuri's hands glided up and down his sides in the most sensual of caresses. The sweats he'd thrown on when he'd gotten home might as well have been air, for he could feel all of Yuri pressing onto his lower body. And he was sure Yuri could feel his own ardor, especially since he had no underwear on.

Lake gasped again. Yuri had slid his hand beneath the waistband of his sweats and encircled him.

"Ah, bolshoi," the Russian said huskily.

Yuri's manipulations were driving Lake insane. He worked Yuri's belt and pants open and slid his hands inside. He squeezed Yuri's now exposed buttocks and pulled him impossibly closer to him. He needed to feel all of the Russian touching him right now. "Please," he gasped.

Yuri removed his hand from Lake and finished removing his pants as Lake quickly shucked his own. Lake looked down needing to see all of Yuri. He was most impressed. No, more than that—enthralled.

Lake looked up. Yuri's eyes were piercing his own. The sexual intensity was almost frightening, yet, incredibly exciting.

Yuri breathed hard. "I cannot help myself. You have a power over me. If this is all I can have, I must have it. Lake, I give myself to you."

Lake was totally overwhelmed and overcome. He had never heard such a declaration. Yet, Yuri's words carried an almost ominous tone. All I can have? What did that mean? Lake did not have time to think about it, for he was being carried now by Yuri to his bedroom and Yuri's lips were locked onto his.

Yuri almost reverently laid Lake on the bed and stared down at him. "You are magnificent. I want to be everything for you this night."

Lake stared up at this ultimate fantasy. Angel or not, Yuri was divine. A supernatural aura seemed to envelop them as Yuri slowly came to Lake. Everywhere their bodies touched brought new sensations, as if each nerve had a life of its own.

Lake realized that he had needed this. He had needed this his whole life. Someone to really care for him. Could this be love? After such a short time? All Lake did know was that, whatever he was feeling, it was for the first time, and he wanted it to go on forever.

"I want us to both share everything," Yuri whispered as his mouth moved over Lake's body.

"Da," was all Lake could say.

And they began to experience each other in ways that Lake thought weren't possible. Physically. Emotionally. Spiritually. They both seemed to have a sixth sense about what pleased the other. Nothing was taboo. Everything was perfect. And when they ultimately joined and climaxed simultaneously, Earth and Heaven shook.

It seemed that the night went on forever, and yet it also seemed to pass in the blink of an eye. Lake didn't remember falling asleep. He just remembered being locked in Yuri's arms.

Which now were gone.

Lake opened his eyes. It was daylight. Possibly, late in the daylight. Yuri was gone. His scent remained. Lake knew it hadn't been a dream, but it had certainly been something otherworldly.

"Yuri?"

Silence.

Panic.

He was alone. He'd been used and discarded.

No. He mustn't think like that. This was the new Lake. Even if Yuri was gone, he would survive. Because now he knew he could. "Thank you, Yuri."

Lake got up and strode to the window looking out over the San Fernando Valley. He felt a nuzzle at his thigh. Sebaka. Russian. Yuri. Fate? Tears came to his eyes as he rubbed the dog's head. He felt love. He felt happy. Happy with who he was. "I love you, Sebaka. And most of all... I love me." He hugged himself and looked up. "And Yuri, wherever and whatever you are, I love you."

"Ya lyublyu vass."

Lake whirled around. "Yuri!"

"Da, golubchik. I hope that no one has binoculars, because you are definitely a vision for the eyes."

Lake was puzzled for a moment, then realized he was naked. "I wanted to be ready for you." And began to exhibit his readiness.

Yuri's gaze became heated. "I would like nothing more, lyublyu. But we have to talk."

Lake's ardor began to wilt.

Then the "new Lake" took charge. He locked his gaze with Yuri's and walked slowly toward him. Lake's desire came back with full vigor. He brought his mouth to Yuri's and pressed himself fully against him. Yuri's arms naturally encircled him, and Lake could feel Yuri's very full hardness pressed up against his own. This man wanted him. Their kiss was just as full and passionate as any from the previous night.

Lake whispered, "You do love me."

"That is what I said before, meelby—Ya lyublyu vass—I love you."

Lake kissed him even more fervently than before and wanted to draw Yuri inside him. He wanted Yuri to be a part of him.

Lake finally broke the kiss. "Let's talk," he said, and drew Yuri to the bed.

"You make it very hard when you are sitting here looking so incredible. And we are on your bed."

"Well, the hard part is not going to go away... possibly ever. I'll pull the sheet over me."

"That will not make a difference. I know what is right there beneath it... " He swallowed hard. "... Waiting for me."

"Would you like to make love?"

"More than my existence."

Lake pulled the sheet away. "Make love to me, lyublyu."

And he did.

Two hours and two orgasms later, Yuri moved his head from Lake's chest and stared up into Lake's deep blue eyes. "I am in trouble."

"I am in heaven. Sorry. Bad choice of words. But apropos nonetheless."

"Heaven, yes. That is my trouble. We are not supposed to fall in love."

"But you have?" Lake was tentative.

"Yes."

"And?"

"I have talked to... I guess you would call them superiors. But really they are not. No one is superior to anyone else."

"Other... angels, then?"

"Da. Other angels. God loves love. God is love. There are no distinctions with love. No genders. No barriers. Love is what it is. And sometimes angels fall in love when they find their eternity partner. But both sides must feel the same and realize it."

Lake could barely breathe, let alone speak. "And... you think I am your eternity partner?"

"Da."

Lake stared into Yuri's glorious gray eyes. "Then there's no problem. I know you're mine."

"I cannot live here on Earth. I have already done that."

"Then I'll go with you."

"That is the problem. You cannot choose to end your life here. You have to leave this existence when it is your time. Otherwise... "

"I'll go to Hell," Lake finished for him.

"Something like that."

"So, where does that leave us?"

"I was sent here to help you and guide you. I have always been around, but had not needed to make myself known to you before this."

"Then why now?" Lake paused. "The movie."

"Da. You were going to choose to make that film. It would have been disastrous for you."

"How do you know?"

Yuri stared at him.

"You're right. I was going to give in."

"It would have changed the entire course of your life. We are assigned good people who have circumstances in their lives to overcome. We watch their life's progress and occasionally give, what you call a nudge, to help you stay on the right path. And very occasionally, we have to make our presence known."

"Then you know what is going to happen to me in my life?"

"Nyet. We are given insight into possible outcomes of certain decisions. You have free will. We are strictly guides. You make your own destiny."

Lake suddenly realized that, somewhere along the way, he had totally accepted the fact that Yuri was, indeed, an angel. He had never been particularly religious, but he did believe in a higher Being and a hereafter. At least he had been right. "But now that I've made the "right" decision, what happens?"

"It is up to you."

"Are you going to stop being my angel?"

"No. I will always be your angel."

"But I want you to be my lover, my partner, my... my eternity mate."

"Lake, you must live out your life. There is a possibility that you will find someone else here in this existence to love." He paused, and Lake could see the raw emotion there. "You should find someone here to share your life. You are a wonderful man and have much to give."

"I know what I want. When I feel strongly about something, as I do about you, I go for it and don't look back. I wanted to leave home and become an actor. And I've done it, in spite of... things."

"Your father, da."

Lake's eyes flared for an instant. "I don't want to talk about him."

"But that is something you need to do. Talk about him and perhaps to him."

"I can't."

"Meelby, you can do anything you want to—if you really want to."

For the first time in his life, Lake knew that he was about to tell someone about his past.

Yuri instinctively put his arm around him. Lake leaned into him.

"My father was—is—a bastard. Nothing I did was ever good enough for him. My mother was smart; she got out early, when I was only three. I sort of remember her, but nothing really stands out. I heard she died when I was ten. She'd never bothered to see me. That hurt some, I guess, but what I really wanted to do was make my father proud of me. I tried some sports, because he wanted me to. I was okay at them but not a star, so he was disappointed. I did pretty well in school, got good grades, but not straight A's, so again my father was disappointed. He used to say I was a loser. Then, I tried out for the school play, my junior year in high school. I got the lead. I was so proud. But my father wasn't. He said acting was for fags. But I loved it. And I knew I was good at it. Opening night came and I was great—at least everyone said I was—and I felt good about it.

"Everyone loved me, but my father. He didn't come to see me. He never came. Sure, he heard from people around town and at work that I had real talent. But he didn't care. I guess that's it. He never cared. About me or anything. Now that I think about it, I don't remember him ever really caring or getting excited about anything. I think he was just existing day to day. He didn't love me. He didn't love anything or anyone. Most of all himself. What was I trying to do? Make a man love me who was incapable of love?" He paused and realized that Yuri had been rubbing his back and shoulders the whole time.

"He was all I had. I never saw any other relatives. He told me we didn't have any, or that they were no good. And I never bothered to find out. I really didn't have many friends. I couldn't bring anyone home because of him, and no one wanted to be around him anyway. They thought he was weird. I had a few people in the theater I hung out with. That's when I realized I was gay. I met this one guy, Greg Jeffries, and we messed around for a while, but that ended when we both went off to college. Another thing my father didn't want me to do, and I had to pay my own way if I wanted to go. I did get an acting scholarship. That helped some, but I still waited a lot of tables." He stopped and stiffened. He had felt the emotion building up and threatening to overwhelm him.

"What is it, dorogoy?"

"I can't."

"Yes, you can. You can do anything." He turned Lake's head to his. "I love you."

That did it. The wall came down. Lake started to cry. Slow tears at first. Then the sobbing came.

The sobbing continued for several minutes and then began to subside. "I'm sorry."

"For what, lyublyu? For being the most wonderful man I have ever met. You are so loving and compassionate. Your father could never realize this."

"Yes. I know that now. Thank you."

"Do not thank me. Thank yourself. You did it. Forgiveness is the greatest virtue."

"Yes. I do forgive him. I pity him. It makes me sad that he could never have feelings, true feelings, for anything or anyone. Even when I finally told him I was gay, the day I left for college, he said to me again that acting was for fags. And I told him I was one. He could only say, 'It figures.' Why didn't I know then that he was dead inside? What makes people like that?"

"God knows," Yuri said with a smirk.

"Right. Speaking of which, doesn't He know about our dilemma here. If He loves love in all its forms, how can he not let us be together?"

"I cannot answer that. Only He can."

"How long do we have here together?"

"I do not know. In our lives here on Earth we are meant to learn many things. That is where an angel's guidance comes in. Some learn what they are supposed to and move on. Others must return and, as you say, try again. It is a mystery and a journey."

"I think I'm confused."

"As you should be."

"Can I tell my friend Drew about you? She is the one person I've met who is truly concerned about me and loves me."

"She is a good person. Yes, you may tell her."

"Can I tell her you're an angel? I mean, are there rules about that?"

Yuri laughed. "No, there are no rules. But do you think you should?"

"If anyone would believe me, she would. I'll be right back. Promise me you won't go anywhere?"

"Da, I promise."

Lake left the room and returned several minutes later, smiling broadly.

"She said that if anyone deserved an angel for a lover, it was me. How cool is that?"

"It is very... cool." Yuri grinned as well.

"She was just glad that I'd found someone who could make me happy." He looked lovingly at Yuri. "And you do. Unbelievably so."

"And you do me."

"She's dying to meet you. Will you do that? Meet her?"

"I will do whatever you want for as long as you want, moi lyublyu."

"I want forever." Lake's eyes misted.

"So do I." Yuri's eyes misted in response.

The intensity of love in the room was palpable. Lake was drawn into Yuri's embrace by a force that only the deepest of lover's have.

Their lips met and their souls joined.

The angel and the actor.

Their lips parted their eyes locked on one another.

Lake breathed, "Can we continue this later?"

"Da. All our laters."

"Come on, Sebaka. Let's go see Auntie Drew."

The dog, who was never far away, rushed to Lake's side.

\* \* \*

They drove in Lake's red Ferrari, his one real indulgence, down Mulholland Drive to Benedict Canyon, their hands linked the entire time, Lake often looking over to see Yuri staring at him with unabashed love. Sebaka, squished but content in the car's almost non-existent back seat, looked on happily.

They came around a blind curve, just before their turnoff, and there, in their lane, was a stalled car and a car coming fast in the opposing lane. Lake swerved to the right to avoid the stalled vehicle.

There was no guardrail, and a four-hundred-foot drop off the side of the road awaited them. Yuri grabbed Lake's hand as they plunged into space.

*  *  *

Lake found his hand still clutched in Yuri's. "What happened?"

"Moi lyublyu, you just saved the lives of a mother and her two daughters."

"The car in the road. I remember. But... we went off the road down into the canyon."

"Da, we did."

"Did you save us?"

"No."

Lake hesitated. "I died?"

"Yes, Lake, on Earth your body is no longer." Yuri felt himself holding his breath.

"Did you make that happen so we could be together?"

"I do not have that capability." Yuri was holding his breath again. "Do you think that I would be so selfish as to deprive you of your life and a chance to find someone else?" The worry on his face frightened Lake.

"No. Never. Actually, I was hoping that you would say yes you had caused the accident. I was so devastated thinking that I would have to wait to run the course of my life to be with you. It would have seemed like an eternity. Do you think God had anything to do with it?" He didn't wait for a response. "I know. God knows."

"The only thing I can say is that God truly loves love. Perhaps, he saw that we were eternity partners and helped us along. I truly do not know. But what is a human life compared to eternity? Such a short time. But I would have wished for you to experience it. It was not to be."

"I don't need to know what happened," Lake said. "Just the fact that it did happen is enough for me. The only thing I will miss is Drew. I hope she's happy and understands."

"From what you have told me, she definitely understands and will be happy for you. And, dorogoy, you will be seeing her again. She is a good person and will receive her just rewards."

Then a look of horror came into Lake's eyes. "Sebaka! Oh my God! Sebaka!" Lake began to wail.

"Hush, lyublyu. It is all right."

"No! I killed him!"

"No, no, lyublyu." Yuri tried to hold Lake.

Then Lake felt something nudge his leg.

He looked down.

Sebaka.

"Oh, Sebaka." Lake hugged the dog fiercely as Sebaka lapped his face.

"Dogs go to heaven, too?" Lake looked up at Yuri, tears of joy in his eyes.

"That was rhetorical, wasn't it?" Yuri slowly smiled.

Lake pulled Yuri into his arms and looked deeply into his Russian angel's gray eyes. "Thank you, lyublyu, for now and for always. I said that right, didn't I?"

"Da, lyublyu. Now and always."

"I love you so much. I'm just wondering if eternity is long enough to be with you."

"Time will tell, lyublyu. Time will tell."

# ARIES

Aries – The Ram

Traits: Adventurous, energetic, pioneering, courageous, dynamic, quick-witted, foolhardy, impulsive, impatient, high sex drive, make passionate lovers, make great leaders, like challenges.

The ghost was back. Dade could feel his presence. How could he not? It was always the same, an encroaching miasma of warmth. It was suffocating. And male. He could almost taste the testosterone.

He had to do something. This had been going on for three months now, ever since he'd moved into his new house. His new house. He'd been so excited to finally have a place of his own. Why he'd chosen Arizona, he didn't know. Something had told him: why not go where it's warm all the time? No more snow and cold. He'd had enough of that. And even though it could get hot here, he liked it. It felt right.

He'd refused to use his trust fund from his parents, at least for the house. He'd wanted to buy it with his own money. Now, however, he had started to dip into the fund. He did need to live. Why was he punishing himself? The money was sitting there. He'd never have to work another day in his life. He just needed to figure out what he wanted to do. Those years hawking software had paid off. Now, maybe, he could really move on with his life and actually have a life. Of course, it would still probably be a life alone. He would never be able to share his life with anyone.

Talk about baggage. He had enough for five people. But his psychiatrist had told him he was getting better and really coming to terms with some of his bigger issues—like using his trust fund. And he no longer pitied himself for not having parents. They had died in a car crash several years ago and had never come to terms with him about being gay. They wouldn't accept it or believe it. From nineteen, when he'd told them, to twenty-five, when they'd been killed, his parents had refused to accept it or discuss it. And it had taken him another ten years to resolve it with himself. They were from another era, another way of thinking, and even if they had lived, they never would have fully gotten it. Some people were just like that. He had certainly met others with similar mindsets. It was just too bad that his parents had been part of that narrow-minded sect.

Then, there were the boyfriends. Ugh! None of them wanted to deal with his problems. That's all he ever seemed to find: the vacuous hunks who wanted to party and have sex all the time. Not that sex was a bad thing. He loved it. But a little compassion to go along with the passion might have been nice. He knew he was good-looking, but never played it up. With his dark hair and dark eyes, and that brooding bad-boy quality about him, dates were never a problem. Relationships? Forget about it.

"Bryan. Why? Why? Why?" he said to the empty air. "Why did it have to be you?" He'd said this a thousand times or more over the past few years. He missed his brother so much. "I need you. I want to talk to you. To see you. To hold you. I want you to tell me everything's going to be all right. I need you... to help me with this damn ghost!"

The cloud of warmth began to dissipate. He could breathe again. He wiped his face and felt moisture from tears he hadn't noticed he had shed. "Dammit! I need help here!"

The silence was deafening. "Maybe I should call someone." A wry smile came to his lips as the tune came into his head. "Who ya gonna call?... Bum bum... Ghostbusters! Bum bum... Ghostbusters!" Was there really a ghostbusters? There were those ghost hunter guys, right?

He mulled it over. People would think he was crazy. "That's stupid. Everybody already thinks I am anyway. That's why you moved way out here to the other side of the country. And that's why you're talking out loud to yourself. Because no one else will listen. Except you, ghostly, whoever you are. Well, you know what? Fuck it! I am gonna call someone. Ghostbusters or whoever. You are not gonna ruin this for me. I can make a life here. Just because others retire here, doesn't mean that I have to. Maybe I'll write or paint or something. And you're not gonna stop me. You hear that, Casper? You are outta here! This is my house. You are gonna stop it with the heat clouds, and the furniture moving, and the doors slamming. That's it! You hear me?" He waited for a response. "Oh, now you don't have anything to say. Are you pouting?"

Crash.

Dade looked down the hall to the foyer closet door.

It was open. A book lay on the floor. The telephone book. Lying open. He slowly walked down the hall to the waiting book and picked it up. It was open to Exterminators. He glanced at a large ad.

HOUSEHOLD PROBLEMS?

WE HANDLE ANYTHING!

ANYTHING!

GIVE US A CALL.

GUARANTEED OR YOUR MONEY BACK!

This was just too weird. "Fine. I'll call them!"

✳ ✳ ✳

The phone rang. "Logan Ryls, household problems. You got 'em? We get 'em."

Logan loved saying this. It always made him smile. And as he did, he gave a wink to his co-worker, Helene, who shook her head and went back to her computer.

"What's your problem?" He listened to the voice on the other end of the line. "Uh huh... Yeah... I see... Uh huh... Yep, we can do that... Your address?" He looked at Helene, listening but not listening. 1377 Adobe Terrace. Nice area... How soon? Let me check our schedule and see when we can make you an appointment."

He heard an, "Oh, brother," from Helene. He winked again at her. "Yes, I understand. It's an emergency. It's getting worse? Violent? We'll try and squeeze you in next week... Today? Well... I'd have to cancel some appointments. That's very generous... Oh, wait a moment, my secretary said we had a cancellation this afternoon. Is two o'clock okay? Cool. I mean, great. My team and I will be there then... You're welcome. Bye-bye."

"Why do you put on such a show?" she said. "It's certainly not for my benefit. I've seen your show, bought the CD, and got the T-shirt, or, in your case, tank top. She was referring to the ubiquitous white wife-beater he habitually wore, and which, she had admitted, he looked great in. Of course, she had also admitted, he realized it too. "We need the work. In case you haven't noticed, you have two employees—and I use that term loosely—who would like a paycheck every now and then. If it wasn't for Don's electrical skills and my plumbing gigs, we'd starve!" Helene stood as she said the last.

A red-headed head popped into the doorway. "Did someone say food?"

Helene pointed a finger at Don. "How do you always know when even the slightest hint of food is mentioned. Maybe you should be a psychic, Don. It would go along with the rest of the crazy things we do here. And I didn't say food. I said starve."

"That's okay." Don grinned. "It's lunchtime anyway."

"You just had breakfast an hour ago," Logan said.

"My point exactly. How about pizza?" Don suggested.

Logan just shook his head. "We had pizza yesterday. I know... 'My point exactly.' You don't have to tell me again."

"But—" Don started.

Logan finished, "It's the best food on the planet. But before you call, I need to tell you guys the news. We have... " He paused for dramatic effect. "A ghost hunt!"

Helene raised a dark eyebrow. "That's what you dramatically paused for? When are you going to give up, Logan? How many of these have we had? And not one has really panned out. You think your new ad is going to cut down on the crazies? No."

"But at least we've gotten some other legit work, I did at least: my three wiring jobs last week... so now I won't starve!" Don added.

"Dear, you'll never starve," Helene said. "And yes, Logan, to your credit we have at least gotten some other work. And by the way, that, 'Got haunt?—We've got the hunt!' ad, was ridiculous."

"It worked for milk and that ad with the hot guy and the baby," Logan said, defensively.

"And maybe if you'd posed half-naked in the ad, we would have done better, too." Helene's sarcasm was apparent.

"Hey, what about me? I could've posed for that." Don stepped up to her.

"Yes, dear, you could have. But Logan is the bodybuilder. Sex sells. Speaking of which, how did your date with the pool-boy kid go?"

"He wasn't a kid. He was twenty-seven!" Logan on the defense again. "Lousy, if you must know. All his brains were in his... trunks."

"You know, Logan, you are my best friend." Don tried to soften the blow. "But why did you expect a twenty-seven-year-old pool boy to have much on the ball? Pun intended. He doesn't even own the business."

"Yeah, I thought about it."

"Yeah, you thought about what he would look like out of those very tight and very revealing Speedos," Helene said. "By the by, does he have any other clothes? He always shows up to your pool in them and leaves in them. Not that he looks bad in them."

"Hey!" Don whined.

"Just stating a fact, dear. What did he wear when you guys went out?"

"Capri pants."

"Oh no."

"Pink."

"Guess he should stick to the Speedos." Helene nodded. "At least they're white."

Don smirked. "Yeah, you hate pink. Big turn off." Don smirked. "Especially for you."

"Don!"

"Hey, Helene, you were there the day Logan jumped in the pool and lost his trunks. Lotta pink showin'. It was pretty hard to hide."

"Incorrigible." She shook her head.

"And proud of it." Don put a hand over his heart. "If he'd been tan all over it wouldn't have been so much pink."

"And if you hadn't been shouting, "Pink! Pink!" the rest of the party wouldn't have known," Logan said.

"You keep telling yourself that... big boy." Don started looking through pizza coupons.

"If you two are done embarrassing me, can we please get down to work? We have to be at this guy's place at two. Don, get the equipment: the handy cam, the EMF, the DVR, the infrared probe, the—"

"Done this before, Logan. It's all in the ghost hunters' room." He emphasized with air quote marks.

"Then get your—" He air-quoted back. "butt moving. We've only got an hour."

Don scooted out the door. "Let's get Dean's pizza today. It's my favorite."

Helene sighed. "Here we go again. Maybe this guy'll be cute, Logan, and you'll get a date. At least you'll get something out of it."

"Sarcasm does not look good on you. One of these days we'll encounter the real thing. Who knows? This may be the one. I believe ghosts are real, and so do you or you wouldn't be here. We've just had some bad luck."

"Five years of it, Logan."

"These things can take a while."

"Like your love life?"

"Whew! What did you eat for breakfast today? Didn't it agree with you?"

"I'm fine. I just don't like to see you get your hopes up too much. Because when you do, you brood for the next week. Not fun for any of us."

"All right. I promise no brooding. And I'm already getting better. I didn't brood over the pool boy."

"Even you knew that had no future beyond one night. The only thing you had in common were good looks." Helene quirked a smile.

Logan smiled back. "That was harsh, but thanks for the compliment."

"I reiterate: incorrigible. You and Don. The only difference is the sexual persuasion."

"Are you sure about that?"

She gave Logan a look he knew all too well. She wanted to throw something at him. "If you... "

He scooted out of the room before she could.

\* \* \*

The front door opened. No one was there. Logan took a quick step back.

"Sorry," a voice said. A male face peeked out around the door. "A little ghost joke." The man stepped forward and extended his hand. "I'm Dade."

Logan stared.

Helene stepped around him and took Dade's hand. "Hi, I'm Helene. This is my husband Don, behind me. And this is our fearless leader, Logan." She elbowed him.

Logan emerged from his trance, and said in a monotone, "Hi, I'm Logan." He extended his hand.

"The Stepford boy," Don volunteered from behind his mass of equipment. "I see trouble."

"Excuse me?" Dade said.

"Don't mind my husband. Sometimes he thinks he's funny. Try to ignore him."

Dade grabbed Logan's still extended hand. "Oh, I'm sorry. I didn't mean to rude." He took the proffered hand. "This is all—" He looked into Logan's eyes. Neither said a word.

Helene broke the awkwardness. "It's very nice to meet you, Dade." She elbowed Logan again.

"It's very nice to meet you, Dade," Logan said, still holding Dade's hand.

"I think I actually saw a spark," Don interjected.

"Don!" Helene whirled around, causing him to stumble back and almost lose his grip on the equipment.

"Did you notice this guy is wearing a matching black wife-beater? Kinda creepy," Don whispered, just loud enough for Logan to hear.

"It's very nice to meet you, Logan," Dade said. His eyes darkened.

"I think I just threw up in my mouth," Don mumbled.

"Stop right now and get inside, or no pizza for a month," Helene ordered. "I'll handle this."

"A month? Jeez. Good luck," Don said, as he awkwardly maneuvered past the two men. "Excuse me, man with very delicate equipment coming through."

That broke the mood. The men's hands and eyes unlocked.

"So what seems to be the nature of your problem, Dade?" Helene began.

Logan tried to recover. "Yes, Dade... " He paused. "What seems to be the nature of your problem?"

Dade started to laugh and looked to Helene. "Do you always prompt him with what to say? It's kind of cute, but it could get annoying."

Logan, finally recovered, said, "I'm so sorry. It's been a long week and—"

Dade saved him. "Ah, an original thought. You can come in now."

Helene brushed past Logan, grabbed his hand, and pulled him inside.

Dade followed.

"Nice," Helene said, as she sauntered down the hall, looking around, before entering into the great room. "Very open."

Following them into the room, Dade said, "Yeah, it's kinda what sold me on it. It's so bright and airy in the daytime. It's now the room I hate the most at night though. Most of the... disturbances seem to happen in here and in my bedroom."

"Your bedroom?" Logan asked. "Uh, could we see it."

"And he's back!" Don chimed in from a corner of the room where he had been setting up some equipment.

"You'll have to forgive Don, Dade. It's a recurring case of Tourette's," Helene said.

"Hey!" Don yelled.

"Pizza," Helene warned.

Don mimed locking his mouth and went back to work.

"It's this way," Dade said and led the way down the hall from the great room.

\* \* \*

Don started after them. "I'm coming, too."

Helene caught his arm, stopping him. "Be good," Helene said.

"I don't wanna miss anything. You know with Logan there's never a dull moment. This might be the one."

"How do you mean that?"

"Both ways. You saw how they looked at each other. He's kind of Logan's type: male. And didn't you get a funky feeling when you were in that grand room?"

"Great room. I hate to admit this—and don't you dare tell Logan—but yes, I kind of got a cold chill in there, even with the sun pouring in... But it could be nothing," she quickly added.

Don falsettoed *The Twilight Zone* theme. "Dee dee dee dee. Dee dee dee dee."

"Stop it. Let's check out the bedroom. Maybe we'll get something there."

"I bet Logan hopes he'll get something there," Don said wryly, and added a, "Heh, heh, heh."

"What am I going to do with you?"

"I keep you amused. And if we don't hurry up, we may be finding out what Logan is going to do with that broody Dade guy."

The door to the bedroom was shut and Don and Helene could hear pounding and shouting from the other side of the door.

"Let us out!" Logan shouted. "This isn't funny."

Don turned the knob and the door opened. "Did you try the knob?" he asked dryly.

"We tried everything. It wouldn't open. We walked into the room and the door slammed shut." Logan paused. "You two didn't do it?"

Helene tilted her head and glared at him. "How long have you known me? Is this something I would ever do? Don, yes. But me? No."

"But we thought that it had to be you," Dade said. "It was such a violent slam and there's no breeze. The ghost is advancing his game."

"Ick. I think I need to eat," Don said.

Dade brushed past them and out the door. "Please follow me. I have some refreshments. I know I could use a drink. Logan?"

"Sure. That would be great."

"Did he use the word refreshments out loud? Nobody talks like that in real life. He's creepy," Don said, as Helene and he lagged back a little behind the men.

"He's being polite. I know you don't recognize that quality. And I can't believe you're standing here casting aspersions on him when he's offered you food. He should be your new best friend."

"Aspersions? Are you haunted, too? And food isn't everything."

"I can't believe those words came out of your mouth."

Don ignored her. "I do have standards."

"Now, I know this place is haunted. Someone has possessed my husband. Let's go eat." Helene grabbed his T-shirt and tugged him along.

Dade actually did have a nice spread of refreshments arranged, Don was quick to note. "I think I take the creepy thing back," he said to Helene.

"Take what back?" Dade had appeared at Don's shoulder.

Don jumped back a full step, dropping the pickle spear he was just about to consume. "Whoa. Sorry." He bent to pick up the pickle and promptly popped it into his mouth.

"Don, must you?" Helene shook her head. "He doesn't like to waste food."

Dade smiled. "There are plates right on the end of the island."

"Oooh, right," Don garbled as he shoved another spear into his mouth and scurried the six feet to the end of the very full, kitchen island, glad to have diverted Dade from his "take it back" comment about him.

* * *

Logan stood watching from the doorway appreciating the kitchen's décor and the lovely set-up Dade had prepared for their visit. What a great host. The food display even had levels. He'd have to take notes for his next party. And this was just casual! Maybe he could hire Dade to cater for him. Focus. He really needed to focus, but it was proving more and more difficult as he became mesmerized by this beautiful man. He was in trouble. Again. But Dade did seem to be interested in him as well, and he also seemed to be pretty intelligent and well adjusted—aside from the haunting thing. He thought they were about the same age, too. A novelty, at least recently.

"That drink? Or how about some food first?" The beautiful man brought Logan out of his reverie.

"Oh, thanks. Drink, I think. Then maybe some food."

"Drinking on an empty stomach? You're not going to get drunk on me, I hope?"

Was there a hint of irony in Dade's voice.

"Bourbon, okay?"

"I have a high tolerance for liquor. I'll be fine. And yes, bourbon's my favorite." He smiled warmly at Dade.

Dade smiled back, bringing an entirely new look to his dark looks, and enthralling Logan even more.

Their eyes locked for a moment, until—

"I think I'm going to hurk," Don mumbled out.

"Something wrong with the food?" Dade turned to him, breaking the tension with Logan.

"Don?" Helene said. "Answer our generous client."

"Uh… uh… .no, everything's great. It's just that there's so much of it. Thanks. Thanks. Everything's great. Is this cheesecake?" He started cutting a large piece. "It's my favorite." He bowed his head in concentration, afraid to meet Dade's eyes.

"Yes, a friend of mine makes them in her little shop in town. Shelley's bakery? It's new. And you can have more than one piece. I'm not sure that one will fit on the plate."

Logan noticed him eye the enormous chunk of cake Don was attempting to maneuver onto his plate.

"I'll make it. Don't worry. Thanks." He started to shovel in a mouthful.

"Enjoy. Oh, sorry, Logan, I'll get that drink. Don? Helene? A drink?"

"Coke," they said simultaneously.

"It's in the refrigerator. I'll—"

Don already had the door open.

"Help yourself. Glasses are—"

"Got 'em," Don said, opening an overhead cupboard.

"Help yourself," Dade added wryly. "Logan, my bar's here in the great room if you want to join me."

Logan followed, saying, "Don, when you're through gorging yourself, make sure you have all the equipment set up. I don't want to chance missing anything. This could be the one."

* * *

"Good luck to us." Dade clinked his glass to Logan's.

Logan appeared to get the double entendre and met his eyes. "Yes. Good luck," he said and sipped. "Nice."

"Basil Hayden. My favorite."

"I think it just became mine, too." Logan sipped again.

"Let me know whatever you need."

"We have everything, and we'll need to know where most of the occurrences have happened. Obviously your bedroom, and in here. Where else?"

"That's mainly it... outside of the foyer, where the—"

"Go ahead and tell me. I won't think you're crazy or anything. Hell, look what I do for a living," Logan reassured him.

"The phone book fell from the shelf in the closet and opened to your ad. That's why I called you," Dade finished.

Logan's face twisted in wonder. "It just fell out of the closet?"

"Actually, it was like it was thrown. You saw the foyer and the closet. It fell a good six feet from the door." Dade dove in now with more confidence, feeling he could trust Logan. "This has been the most violent activity. Before, it was mostly lights flickering, doors closing, breezes with all the doors and windows closed... and the heat."

"What do you mean?"

"It's like a presence seems to come into the room. It's almost a suffocating warmth. And it's male. The air seems to radiate, I guess, with that, well, you know, very male presence." He couldn't believe his awkward description and lack of vocabulary.

Logan was looking directly into his eyes. "I know." Eyes lingered for a moment. "We'll definitely need a couple of more TIDCs."

"Those would be?"

"Thermal imaging digital cameras. They detect abnormal changes in temperature" Logan said.

"Wow. I guess you are like those Ghost Hunter guys."

"Without the TV show."

"Too bad. With your looks and body, I'm sure you could make it a ratings hit. Those guys are interesting, but as far as being attractive... well... "

"Thanks," Logan said. He blushed.

"Sorry. I didn't mean to embarrass you. But you are a great-looking guy."

"Thanks. Again. I blush easily. And I'd tune into your show, too."

Dade burst out laughing. "That has got to be the most original and best compliment I've ever gotten. Thank you. And that's the first time I've really laughed in a long time. I don't laugh much, but it feels good to do it. With so much going on: moving, the house, the ghost, I've not had much of a life. Who would have thought it would take a hot ghost hunter to make me realize it?"

"You should laugh more. You've got a great smile. It makes your whole face light up. Hang around the 'Don and Helene Comedy Hour' for a while and that should do it."

"Maybe I will. They seem like quite the pair. Have you known them long? And would you like another drink?" He'd noticed Logan's now empty glass.

"Most of my life. We moved out here from upstate New York. Not a lot was happening there professionally or personally— for me anyway. And no thanks. I need a clear head." He set the empty on the bar. "They're great friends, and speaking of which, I think we need to head back to the office for another TIDC. He winked at Dade, and a K2 meter. I'm sure Don didn't bring that."

"K2—"

"Ghost communicator. Maybe your guy will try to talk to us."

Dade nodded. "I hope you're ready for all this."

"My whole life." Logan looked at him and smiled slightly.

\* \* \*

"So, lover boy, what happened?" Don asked Logan on the drive to the house in the van. "What did you talk about? Helene wouldn't let me listen in." Don hmphed.

"Of course not. You know he'll tell us everything anyway."

"Yeah, but it's more fun to listen in. It's sneakier. Did you talk about us and say what a great job we do, and how we wouldn't be surviving it wasn't for my expertise and electrical prowess?"

Logan laughed. "Something like that. He's really a great guy. Hot looking, friendly, but I kind of get he's got some history. Some stuff that he's trying to hide. I mean, other than the ghost thing, which he was pretty forthcoming with. It's like he's got something bad or tragic in his past. He didn't say so, but I got a feeling."

Don hmphed again. "I just bet you got a feeling. So, he likes you, huh? You two gonna—"

"Don!" Helene scolded him from the back seat. "Don't encourage him. I agree, Logan. He does to appear to be more than meets the eye. You need to be careful. A man that good-looking and intelligent—not to mention apparently wealthy, and still single... I'm just not sure."

"I'm still single," Logan reminded them.

"Her point exactly," Don said.

"Thanks, B.B.," Logan said, referencing their childhood nickname for "best buddy."

"Anytime. I calls 'em likes I sees 'em."

"Really, Logan," Helene said. "It's obvious you're both attracted to one another, but you need to take it slowly."

"Fat chance," Don said. "You know him. Joust-and-jump Logan. Hey, that was really clever. I just made that up, the alliteration. I'm so good. When are we gonna eat? I'm hungry. All this drama and spookiness has made me famished. There's a Mickey D's coming up."

"Fine. Drive-through okay? We can eat at the house." Logan was happy for the change of subject. "Don, you want the usual?"

"Yeah, but add a quarter-pounder with cheese. I think I need the fortifying. Sounds like it might be a long night."

* * *

They got back to Dade's house around 8:30 P.M. The sun had set, but the September temperature was still a hundred degrees.

Don, loaded down with equipment, pushed his way past Logan and Helen as soon as Dade opened the door. "Out of the way, pack mule coming through."

"What's all this?" Dade asked.

"More variations on a theme. Meters, cameras, etc., Logan said.

"And they made me carry it all," Don said as he unburdened himself of the sacks and cases.

"You grabbed it all, so quit complaining," Helene reminded him.

"We want to make sure we cover everywhere so we don't miss anything" Logan said. "You have a big house. And even though it's all one level, it's a lot of area to cover. Tell us where all the hauntings, or disturbances if you will, have occurred. We'll separate and sit in the most likely rooms to have contact and let the cameras handle rest. We'll check them periodically. I hope you napped while we were gone. You might not be able to sleep later."

"As a matter of fact, I did. I didn't want to miss this. It's my ghost after all."

"I was hoping you'd say that." Logan nodded. "He—I guess we'll call him that since you seem to be convinced it's a man—will probably be more apt to show up if you're around. From what you've said, it's you he's haunting and not the house."

"I'm all yours," Dade volunteered, hands out at his sides.

"I'll bet," Don mumbled as he fiddled with a tripod.

"Dear?" Helene said. "Don't you think we need another camera in that corner?" She pointed to the back wall of the great room.

"No, this has got it covered," he said, affixing the camera's position.

"Good. Then you should be stationed here, I think. Logan?"

"That's fine," Logan said as he and Dade untangled a cable. "Do you want foyer, Dade's bedroom, or one of the other rooms?"

"I think the foyer for starters." Then she said, "Maybe you should take his bedroom."

"Oh, boy. Here we go." Don muttered. He put on headphones and began fumbling with some knobs on the device in front of him.

"You got something?" Dade said, oblivious of the implication.

"Nope. Tuning up. Gettin' it all ready." Don returned, slightly embarrassed at being heard.

"Yes, dear. Watch the volume level and your comments." Helene smiled.

"Dade, could you grab the rest of that stuff and bring it with me to the bedroom?" Logan said, arms full.

"You sure you can you handle it all?" Don said asked and winked at Logan.

"Sure. There's not a lot," Dade said.

"You'd be surprised," Don said. "Be gentle, though. Delicate equipment. You don't want to hurt anything."

"Don't worry. I won't." Dade walked down the hall, following Logan.

"You get genuine pleasure out of doing that don't you?" Helene said after the men had left the room, shaking her head.

"You bet. He didn't suspect a thing. I wish Logan had heard it. He would have been proud. He appreciates my subtle inferences and witty repartee."

"Then maybe you should have married him. Because your witty repartee is eluding me. Get to work. We are being paid for this, you know."

"I know. I will. I need to run to the kitchen for a snack. Be right back." He dashed off.

* * *

Put that equipment anywhere that's convenient," Logan told Dade.

Dade set everything on the bed. "Even though I'm actually being haunted, this stuff has always fascinated me. What does this do?"

Logan glanced at the machine he was pointing to. "It measures EVPs—electronic voice phenomena. Hopefully we'll get some results with it." And with this guy is the K2 meter." He tapped it as he set it down on Dade's dresser. "Is it okay here?"

"Sure, let me clear my stuff out of the way." He grabbed a couple bottles of cologne, some papers, but left a picture frame.

"Uh, who's the guy in the picture with you?" He noted their arms around one another. "A friend?... Boyfriend? He's nice looking." He tried not to show too much interest.

Dade's face darkened. "My brother, Bryan. He died."

Shit. Logan wanted to crawl into a hole. "I'm sorry. An accident? You were close?"

"Very. It was my fault."

"Oh. I... I'm really sorry. I didn't mean to pry."

"You didn't know. It was eight years ago this month."

Logan saw a lost-boy look come over his face. His heart went out to him.

"We were all each other had. I loved him so much." His voice broke on the last word, and he turned to Logan. "I'm sorry. I don't normally talk about it—except to my therapist. I don't really have anyone to talk to anyway."

"That's fine. I'm a good listener. Anytime you want to talk."

Dade gave him a slight smile. "I really think you mean that. Thank you. I just might." He looked Logan up and down. "You're more than just a good-looking hunk, you know. You've got a brain and a heart, too. How come you're not with someone?"

"I—"

"That was so rude of me. I apologize. I didn't mean to imply there had to be something wrong with you. I—"

"It's all right." He laughed. "I'll own up to it. I haven't found the right guy yet. It's probably because, as Don would say, I'm using the wrong head when I go after a guy. I always get the hot-looking, vacuous type."

Dade chuckled. "And if you used the word 'vacuous' to them, I'm sure the relationships were short."

"Minutes, for some of them."

"Ouch. Minutes?"

"For them. Not me."

"Good to know."

"Because—"

Don burst into the room. "Have you seen the—Oh, there it is." He thrust between the two of them and grabbed an odd-looking cable. "Did I interrupt anything? Sorry. I'll knock next time... or not." He walked out of the room. "Oh, and Dade? You're out of pickles."

They looked at one another and started laughing.

"I'll be sure to stock up." Dade called out after Don He turned back to Logan. "He's... fun."

"Yeah. He and Helene are my best friends. They'd have to be. They've been through all the various loser boyfriends I've had. And they never hesitate to let me know exactly how they feel about them."

"And?"

"Let's just say that if I were a baseball pitcher, I would be the greatest ever strike-outs every time."

"Nice analogy. Painful, but to the point."

After a momentary silence, Dade said, "My boyfriend situations, or lack thereof, have been similar. Looks, but no substance. Or, more often, if there is a possibility, they turn tail and run when I mention I'm in therapy and have issues I still need to work through."

"Bah. Like there's one gay man out there who doesn't have some kind of issue to deal with. Just lame excuses. Nobody wants to commit. Then they all wait till it's too late. They've lost their looks, don't have anything else to offer, and they're still going after the young buff guys." He thought for a moment. "Did I just describe myself?"

Dade laughed again. "I don't think so. Even if you lose your great looks, you've got a lot more going for you."

"Thanks for the vote of confidence. We'll see if you still think the same thing after you get to know me."

"Will I get the chance to know you?" Dade now had a look of concern on his face that Logan hadn't seen yet.

"Yeah, if you want." He smiled. "I'd like that."

Dade smiled back.

"But first we've got a ghost to find." Logan said.

"Is it all right if I stay in here with you? I'd love to watch you work and learn all about this."

"Sure. I'll be happy to show you. I was going to ask if you would stay. Since the ghost seems to be haunting you, your presence should help a lot."

"Great. If you need me to do or get anything, I'm all yours."

Logan had a great comeback for that, but kept himself in check. There was always time later. He had a job to do. Maybe his first honest-to-God haunting!

\* \* \*

Over the next few hours, Logan went back and forth between the rooms, checking devices, meters, levels. Nothing extraordinary. He was becoming a little discouraged. He had let Helene run home about 11:00 to feed and let out their dogs and cats. Just after midnight she returned, saying all the "babies" were fed and fine. Logan went back to the bedroom, where Dade had been overseeing the monitors, after Logan had instructed him on what to watch for. Dade had picked things up quickly and seemed quite eager. And Logan was encouraged by his interest in it all.

"Any ghostly disturbances, pardner?" Logan affected his best cowboy imitation.

Dade playfully joined in. "Nope, pardner. They's nothin' in them thar hills."

"Well, welcome to the world of ghost-hunting. It's a lot of this. But when you get that first blip or odd sound on the monitor, it's quite the rush."

"Have you had a lot of hauntings?"

"Not really. Mostly it's debunking. We've had a few possibles, but never really anything that was a definite-can't-explain-it-no-way haunting. But I always have hope. If the Ghost Hunter guys can do it, why not us? Ghosts are not exclusive. At least I don't think so. I've never heard they only show up when they know they're going to be on TV."

Dade laughed, something he'd been doing a lot since Logan and crew had arrived. It felt good. Maybe there was hope for him yet. "A ham ghost?"

"Right. But then again those guys are paid to go to those purported haunted sights. The bankroll helps. I have to admit, it's really more of a sideline for us. We make our money from repairs and plumbing. Which isn't bad, just not very glamorous."

"Or what you really want to do."

"You got it."

"You're not that hard to read... at least as far as your love for the hunt is concerned," Dade said.

"I'm not hard to read anyway. I'm pretty much 'what you see is what you get.'"

"I like what I see."

Logan felt the air around them get warmer. A strange warmth. Was it just him? He started to sweat. He could smell the masculine musk in the air. He needed to slow down and focus. He was here to do a job, not score another date. But Dade was different, in so many ways. Sexy? Absolutely. Mysterious? Definitely. He could see the agony of a troubled past in Dade's eyes. He'd said he was seeing a therapist to help him through things, but he didn't get the feeling it was about being generally messed up, but more about something unresolved. Something he needed to finish. Hell, he had his own problems: a struggling business, one nightmare boyfriend after another, with no prospects in sight. At least—maybe—until now. There was something compelling about Dade, something real, something honest. And it was obvious Dade was interested, but it didn't feel like he was looking for a one-time thing. If he went for it now, he had to be prepared for the long haul. God knew, that's what he'd really been looking for. He wanted what Don and Helene had. And they did seem to have a lot in common. Age, for one. Finally. Being a Twinkie magnet was nice for the ego but was getting old fast.

This guy seemed to be the real deal. Did he really have anything to lose? He opened his mouth to speak. Here goes.

"I like what I see, too."

The smell of their commingled sweat now permeated the air, their faces inches apart.

Logan sniffed the air. "I'm kind of sweaty. Maybe I should take a shower."

"No. It's fine. Maybe, after." Dade inched closer.

"After what?"

"This."

Dade's mouth pressed onto his. Lips and tongues began their explorations. Their arms remained at their sides, all sensation concentrated in one area: lips, tongues, mouths.

Logan felt hands at his waist, tugging his tank top from his jeans, up over his chest. Their mouths parted for a moment. He sucked in air. The shirt made its way over his head and stopped, pinning his arms together above his head. Dade entwined one hand in the shirt, making a noose for his wrists.

"Keep them there," was whispered in his ear. As if he wanted to move.

The tongue began at his ear and began to trail down the side of his neck. His head began to spin as he became lost in sensation. Under his chin now. Momentarily back up to his lips—a tickling sensation. Back down his neck, across his shoulder. Then, quickly, up to his elbow. Now, a slow descent back down his exposed triceps. Biceps. Under his arm. Lingering. Exploring. The sensitivity. The slickness of his tongue as it licked and tasted. The stimulation caused him to writhe uncontrollably under the exploration. Suddenly, the tongue back to his mouth. Salt and sweat. The moisture caressed his lips and tongue. Logan began to bring his arms down to embrace him.

"Not yet. There's more."

Dade repeated the same excruciatingly erotic ministrations to Logan's other arm. Logan had never known such a feeling. It was almost as if he couldn't stand it. He wanted to cry out with the pleasure. Then, as their lips parted again—

"My turn?"

Logan couldn't wait to return the favor, to taste as he'd been tasted. To explore this incredible man. "I think I'd like to lay you down for this. Besides, I think my legs might give out."

Dade smiled. "Whatever you want. I'm all yours." This time when he said it, the meaning was clear.

And it was almost Logan's undoing. He wanted to rip Dade's clothes off and attack him, but knew this slow, erotic torture would be so much better and so much more fulfilling—unlike anything or anyone he'd ever experienced. And he wanted it to last. He would make it last. He wanted to give Dade the same exquisite pleasure he'd gotten. More even. He wanted to give him everything he had. This was going to be it. He was going to go for it. It just felt so right.

He shoved Dade back onto the bed and wrenched the shirt from his waist, his own now discarded. He sat astride Dade's waist and could feel the obvious arousal pressing into him. He held his body over Dade's, their eyes locked, both his arms holding Dade's above his head. He slowly brought his naked chest down to meet Dade's own, knowing that the shock of their two bodies touching would be an incredible pleasure and torture.

Bodies met.

They gasped.

How could one body feel so different from another? Logan's mouth sought Dade's in a mad devouring.

Their bodies squirmed against one another. Their arousals ached to rip through the denim and join together.

But not yet. Logan needed to return the favor. His mouth began to move. He made his own journey over Dade's naked torso. Neck. Shoulders. Arms. He feasted.

Dade moaned. And every time he did, Logan would claim his mouth and let him taste and savor. To let him experience what he was experiencing. To share. That's what sex— No. Making love was all about. The sharing.

Chest now. Back to mouth.

Lower.

He stood. Stared. Enjoyed. Watched the moisture slowly evaporate from the etched, muscled body where his tongue had just been.

He reached for the button on Dade's jeans, knowing that as soon as he did this his life would change forever. Who was he kidding? His life had already changed the moment the door had opened that afternoon and he had stared into those dark, arresting eyes.

He slid the zipper down and removed the jeans. Nothing underneath. Logan had known that. He stood and stared once again. He had also known Dade would be perfect everywhere. He was.

"My turn." Dade's voice rose slightly. "Please."

Logan nodded, almost imperceptibly. He was anxious. He was excited. He was scared, but comforted, sensing that Dade felt the same way.

They switched positions. Logan lay there as Dade slowly slid off his pants and revealed him.

Both now naked and fully aroused, Dade stared down at him. "Perfect."

Logan could only smile, as his own voiced thought came from his lover's lips. Then, Dade slowly began to descend onto him and their bodies and souls became one.

Perfect indeed.

\* \* \*

Logan had lost track of time. Hours could have passed. They lay across the bed, their foreheads pressed together, arms around one another. A slight space between their bodies allowed the cooling air to dry their sweat.

"Logan!" A blood-curdling yell.

Don.

They both grabbed their jeans and flew down the hall to the great room.

Naked with their pants held in front of them, they could only stare in amazement at the sight before them. This room had now become stifling, the air thick.

A lamp was on near them, bathing the rest of the room in a dim light, temporarily blinding them. Their eyes began to adjust and they saw—

Don cowered in a far corner of the room, his hand held out in front of him, warding off... A book?

A book was circling the air in front of Don. Helene appeared from the hall, coming from the foyer. "Don! What is wrong with—" She froze, mouth open.

"I don't believe it," she said. "You were right." Which didn't seem to be directed at anyone in particular. "This place is haunted. Don, are you all right? Are you hurt?"

"No, but get this freaking thing away from me." He tried to bat at the book, which easily dodged his futile attempt. "This is your fault, Logan. We should have called you an hour ago, when we started to get some funky readings on the TIDC, but nooo." Helene said to leave you two alone. Give you a chance." He gestured at Helene, as if trying not to be as scared as he seemed. "You were the one who wasn't so sure about Dade. I liked him right off the bat." The book flew toward his head. He ducked. The book passed over him, narrowly missing. "Hey! Well, all right, maybe I did say something about being creepy."

Logan and Dade stared in disbelief. Still naked.

"Don, how can you have a discussion like this? Logan said. "We're being haunted! By a ghost. A real, live ghost!"

Don gulped. "Probably not live, Logan."

"You know what I mean. Are the cameras running?"

Don tsked. "Please. Give me some credit. I'm not one of your air-head, pool boys."

Dade nudged him. "Pool boys?"

"One. One pool boy. Thanks, Don."

"Well, the others might as well have been pool boys. They all had the same single-digit IQ." He laughed, keeping the, now hovering, book in sight. "Of course, you only were interested in their single digit."

"Enough, already! Don't you think we have something bigger here in front of us?" Logan wanted to bite his tongue and take the question back, knowing what was coming. Too late.

"Well, from what I can see, you've certainly got something bigger in front of you." Don gloated at his wit.

"Don, please." Helene said. "Of course, if you two wouldn't mind putting your pants on, maybe we could accomplish something here."

"I think they already have," Don said.

"Watch that book, Don," Helene said, turning her back.

"No worries there."

The men quickly put on their pants. Don said, "Well, Logan I think you've found your match. He's about your size."

"Don!" Helene yelled down the hall, her back still to them.

"As I've said before, I calls 'em likes I sees 'em."

"Has he always been like this?" Dade asked, adjusting himself.

"You wouldn't have to do that if you wore underwear," Don interjected.

Helene growled. The men both cocked an eyebrow at him.

"Only an observation," Don continued. "Of course, given your... abnormalities, it wouldn't matter anyway."

Logan gave Don a look of disdain. "Yes, Dade, he's always been like this."

"He must be fun at parties," Dade observed.

"Trust me, he's not." Helene, who had now turned around, said.

"Whoa," Don called out. "It's coming after me." The book began to move to his left, herding him from the corner. He started to cross the room to where Helene stood. "I take the back the abnormality comment," he said to the book. "They're normal. Really. Just got a little more than the rest of us guys. It's a gay thing, I think." The book plunged at him. "Sorry, I was kidding. Geez, Logan, this ghost is sensitive. Maybe it's one of your old boyfriends."

The book made another lunge at him and Don ran behind Helene.

"My hero," she said. "It serves you right. I know it won't change a thing, but at least for now, you got a little comeuppance."

The book drifted toward the men, and as it did, Logan noted, "It's The Bible."

Dade grasped Logan's arm. "It's Bryan's," he said barely above a whisper. "It was in my bottom dresser drawer."

The book fluttered to the ground. Opened. The pages began to flip backwards to the beginning. Deuteronomy. Numbers. Leviticus. Exodus. Genesis. It stopped. The pages began to turn one at time now. The ghost was looking for something.

Genesis 4:2-8.

The page began to tear slowly, right above the verses, and Dade read aloud:

"And Cain walked with Abel his brother

And it came to pass, when they were in the field,

That Cain rose up against his brother, and slew him

And the Lord said unto Cain,

Where is Abel, thy brother?

And he said, I know not:

Am I my brother's keeper?"

The verses were torn from the book.

Dade sat back on the floor. Stunned. "Bryan?"

The pages flipped furiously to the Book of Revelation. There was a piece of paper inserted here. Dade hesitantly withdrew it. His fingers trembled. "I've never opened this book since he... since the night... " He set the paper down.

Logan sat next to him and put an arm around him. "It's all right. Tell me." Don and Helene had also silently made their way to the two men. Don had an arm around Helene.

"Our parents were killed in a car crash, years ago. I was twenty-five, Bryan twenty-two. I'd come out to my parents when I was nineteen. They didn't get it or understand it—or even want to understand it. They were from a different era, a different upbringing. Their son couldn't possibly be homosexual, let alone both their sons. Yeah, my little brother was gay, too. They never found out about him, and I made sure they never suspected. He wanted to tell them. Boy, did he want to. We had many a knockdown-drag-out over that. But, ultimately, he listened to me. He always listened to me. I didn't want him to go through what I was going through, to see the looks in their eyes. It hurt so much... and if it wasn't for Bryan—" His pain was obvious.

"It's okay," Logan said, squeezing him reassuringly. "I'm here."

Those simple words seemed to help him continue. "I know." He put his hand over Logan's. "My parents were out at some soiree or other. They were very socially connected. They were driving home. My father always loved to drive. Sports cars. Fast. That night it had been raining. The police said it was probably oil on the road, and along with the rain... There was a bridge on the highway. The police also said maybe a little too much alcohol. But the car spun, hit the guard rail, and went up and over. That was it."

He leaned into Logan's still shirtless chest. Logan shared his warmth, hoping it would comfort and encourage him. He sensed Dade ready to talk about it. What had this man done to him?

"Bryan was inconsolable for weeks. I think a large part was because he'd never told them he was gay. He felt like they never really knew who he was. I tried to tell him that at least they went without having the burden of two gay sons hanging over their heads. They never would have been able to deal with it. In six years, they'd never really accepted me. I think I finally got through to him that it was selfish on his part to want them to know something that would only hurt them. I think he resolved that with himself, even if he didn't like it or agree with it. I also know that it hurt him deeply to see how they'd reacted to me. He was very sensitive." He started to choke up again. There was a small sniff from behind them.

"You don't have to go on," Logan said.

"Oh yes he does," Don said.

"Don, show some sensitivity," Helene said.

"I am. He had me at "Am I my brother's keeper? You heard me sniffle."

Dade gave a small laugh. "I get why you keep him around. I like him. He's a good friend. I hope they both will be to me, too. Whatever happens? If there is to be a future together, I have to tell you the rest." He looked up into Logan's eyes.

"Please," Logan said. "I want there to be a future with you. Tell me. I'll understand."

Don and Helene moved a little closer, as if expecting Dade to whisper.

"Bryan and I lived together after that. We dated people, double-dated, spent time with just each other. We got along great. We had all the money we would ever need from our parents—though I didn't want it. But fortunately, I'd formed my own little—and if I do say so—very successful software company with Bryan as my partner. Everything was great. Well, except for the fact that we couldn't find anyone serious. The money thing always got in the way. We never knew if guys were interested in us for us or for the money. That part sucked."

"Yeah, I bet," Don said.

"Shh," came from both Helene and Logan.

"Whenever Bryan and I would go out, we would always flip to see who would be the designated driver. We could have one drink as the driver, but that was it. Occasionally, we'd both decide to drink and then we'd take a cab. That night, almost exactly eight years ago, Bryan and I had an argument over who would be the driver. There was some guy going to be at this party that Bryan liked, and he wanted to have fun. But I won the toss. I told him it would be better if he had all his wits about him if he really wanted to impress this guy. So, we went. It was a great party and I was drinking—a lot, I think—and Bryan had struck out with the guy. He drove home. On the way, we argued about the guy a little bit. I think I said the guy wasn't good enough, or cute enough, or something. And he said that I'd tried to sabotage him. I do remember talking to the guy, but not much else.

He didn't impress me. And I certainly wouldn't have tried to sabotage him. The events after that are still kind of a blur. I remember headlights coming straight at us as we came up a hill not far from home. Then screaming. Then the hospital. We were hit head-on. A drunk driver, funny enough. I was thrown from the car. Bryan wasn't. The driver, of course, survived; Bryan didn't. It was instantaneous, they said. But not for me. If I'd only given in, it would have been me driving. Me. Not him. Not Bryan."

He looked away from Logan.

Logan turned his face to Dade, trying to convey all the understanding, sympathy and... love that he could. "You couldn't know," he said tenderly. "No one knows the future. We live our lives and make choices. Sometimes right, sometimes wrong. It comes with being human. If I tried to second guess all the wrong choices I've made—"

"We'd be here all night." Don brushed a hand over his cheek. Helene brushed her hand over his other one. "Wait. We are here all night." Helene gave Don's cheek a little slap.

Logan pointed to the paper on the floor. "Dade, I think you need to read that."

"Would you read it for me?"

"You sure?"

"I'm sure."

"Dear Dade," he began. "It's a letter to you."

"Master of the obvious." Don. "Sorry. Read on, Logan."

"There is no way I'll ever be able to tell you what a wonderful brother you've been to me. And I don't know how to tell you this, so I have to write it. Please don't hate me. I'm going to go away soon. Far away. You'll never find me. Don't even try. This is the best thing I can do for you and for me. I can't stay. I know this is selfish of me, but hey, someday I knew I'd have to do something on my own. Well, this is it. I don't have long to live. Weeks, maybe.'"

Dade clutched Logan's thighs. The tears in his eyes began to fall. "I knew something was wrong. I knew it. He was having these stomach cramps... He said it was bad sushi, or crab—it was always some excuse. He said he went to the doctor, and the doctor told him it might be food allergies. I believed him. What an idiot I was. I... Read the rest, Logan."

Logan brushed his hand across Dade's damp cheek. "All right." He continued,

"So, I'm going to use some of our hard earned cash and blow it on whatever I want. I hope you get over Mom and Dad. No disrespect, but they were narrow-minded idiots. You're one of the good guys, and certainly the greatest brother a guy could ever want. I know you love me with all your heart, and if you really do love me—and mean it—you'll do this for me. You will go out and find some incredible man who can appreciate you and who is worthy of you. He's out there. I know it. You'll know it when you find him. Let yourself be open to it. I beg this of you. On our gay-brotherhood-ship, I ask this one thing of you. Be happy. Be happy, for both of us.

I would have done this for you. You know I would. And if you don't do this one thing for me, I swear I will haunt you till you do.

I'll love you forever,

—Bryan"'

An almost unnatural silence pervaded the room.

"I can't, Bryan. I'm sorry," Dade said through his tears. "I'm sorry, too, Logan. I shouldn't have done this. It's not right. I can't." He extricated himself from Logan's arms and got up. "I'll send you your check." He wiped his face. "Please, don't say anything. Leave me alone." Then added to himself, "It's what I deserve."

"What you deserve?" Logan said.

"Please. I'm begging you. Go."

Don, strangely silent, broke their locked gazes by taking Logan's arm and leading him toward the door. Helene followed, also silent.

\* \* \*

As the front door closed...

CRASH!

The bedroom.

Dade dashed down the hall.

He stood in the doorway. His dresser was lying on the floor, face down. The picture of him and Bryan lay face up on the middle of the bed. He went to the bed and picked up the photo. The air in the room, once again, was thick and heavy. Bryan was here.

Dade held the picture to his bare chest. It was strangely warm.

"What do you want from me? I'm sorry, Bry. I should have known you were sick. It's my fault. I should have known. I should have done something. I know you brought me here. You gave me all those signs to move out here. To meet Logan. And yes, he's great. I think I love him. But I can't do this to him. It's not fair."

The tears came again. "He deserves somebody better than me. I have so much to make up for. He could never love me. It would never work; I'm too messed up. It should have been me, Bry, not you. You were the perfect one. Even Mom and Dad thought so. I think I've come to terms with them, now, but I'll never get over you."

He gulped and swallowed, then noticed one of Logan's notebooks, which he must have dropped on the floor, begin to flip its pages.

It stopped on a blank page. A pen floated to the paper and began to write. Dade bent down to read aloud as the pen moved:

My dearest brother, you are an idiot. No one can ever predict what is in store for us in life. My time is over. Now it's yours. Why do you think I'm here? You have done so much. You made my time on this earth wonderful for me. I wouldn't have changed a thing. Life is meant to be enjoyed to its fullest. We are here for such a short time as it is—for some, shorter than others. A little joke. This is your time!

I'm here to make you realize it. With Logan. He's perfect for you. You know it. You need to move on and finally have the life you deserve. You can't blame yourself for things that are beyond your control. I didn't. And you're smarter than me. Do you want me to be happy and move on? Then you have to, too. It's not like I won't see you again. So give yourself a break. Go after him. Make me proud. Be happy.

The pen stopped.

Dade's tears didn't. "All right, Bry. I get it. I guess I needed a little wake-up call. I must sound pretty pathetic. I guess I've been hiding in self-pity and guilt. Okay, I'll give it shot—that is if I haven't scared him off already."

"I'm a ghost hunter. I don't scare easily," Logan said from the doorway.

"Logan!" Dade spun around to see him. "How long have you been there?"

"The whole time. They call that automatic writing. Very cool."

Then, the picture Dade still held was yanked from his arms. It circled the air and floated to Logan, nudging him toward Dade. Logan reached for the picture and held it.

"I guess that means I'm right, and you approve," he said to the hovering notebook.

The air started to get lighter.

"I wish you didn't have to leave, Bryan. I want you stay. At least I know at some point, I'll see you again. Thank you, little brother. Thank you for this amazing man. And thank you for giving me back my life. I'll always love you."

"I don't know whether to bawl or barf," Don whispered to Helene from the hallway just outside the door.

There was a loud pop from the other room. Don rushed out and returned moments later. "It was just a light bulb exploding. And yes, Logan, I got it on tape. You know this haunting thing is going to put us on the map. And, Dade, you can thank Helene and me later for making sure Logan didn't make the biggest mistake of his life. I assume you're going to join us?"

"If you'll have me?" He looked into Logan's eyes with hope and expectation.

"Every way I can think of," Logan said.

"Eew! I so did not need to hear that," Helene said. "It's bad enough that tonight I've gotten to see every inch of both of you stark naked."

"Every inch," Don added.

"That's it, Don. No pizza for a month! Now, come on, let's leave them alone. I'm sure they have a lot to talk about. We can retrieve everything tomorrow."

"You know they're not going to be talking," Don said. "And that's not fair, no pizza. I'm sure you realize my position. Hey, I just had a great idea. We could have a great new show: Gay Ghost Hunters! Two hot gay guys, you two. And one, hot, incredibly funny, straight guy."

"Ahem!"

"Oh, and one hot, straight, married girl," Don quickly added.

"Yeah, we'll see how long the married part lasts. Come on, stud."

"Think about it, guys. See you tomorrow. Don't do anything I wouldn't do." Don hit his head. "I mean, do everything I wouldn't do. Have fun."

"Are you sure you're ready for this?" Logan looked skeptically at Dade as Don exited.

"Are you kidding? I can't wait." They walked into the bedroom, silently, their hands clasped, and sat on the bed.

"Logan, I know this has been a lot to take in. You can't possibly know what to think right now."

"I have never been surer of anything... or of anyone in my life. Before all of this haunting thing started, I knew something extraordinary was about to happen to me when I answered your phone call. You are extraordinary. I realize my whole life has been leading up to this, and to you. When it's right you know it. I know it. I love you."

Dade smiled. "I guess I knew too when you first showed up at my door all Stepfordy and hot-looking. You made me laugh again and brought light back into my life, as clichéd as that sounds. It's true. And I have to say that even without Bryan's help, I think we would have found each other. Of course, I'm grateful for that, too. Now, I know that Bryan's all right, and he knows that I'm all right. All right with you, and in love with you."

They kissed.

Another light bulb popped.

# ABOUT THE AUTHOR

Lance Taubold is the recipient of the IBPA Ben Franklin Award for BEST FIRST NON-FICTION for ON TWO FRONTS.. He has been an entertainer for 25 years, performing at the MET Opera, on Broadway and on television for 5 years on the soap opera "General Hospital." As a writer he has written for Envy Man magazine, both as a fiction writer and book reviewer. His first novel RIPPER A LOVE STORY was written with author Richard Devin.

Taubold is the author of the gay, paranormal romance series: ZODIAC LOVERS BOOKS 1-5.

Taubold has been a contributor to all of the award-winning NEVER FEAR horror anthologies, the UNCHARTED WORLDS-XENO ENCOUNTERS sci-fi anthology and has romance stories in ROMANTIC TIMES: VEGAS, and THE HAUNTED WEST. His next release is the gay romance, murder mystery MAGIC, MURDER AND MISTLETOE. He is currently writing a paranormal romance series with New York Times Bestselling author Heather Graham.

## Never Fear Series

*Indie Book Award Winner*

New York Times bestselling authors, Heather Graham, F. Paul Wilson, Jon Land, Michael Stackpole, Matthew Costello, William F. Nolan and award-winning, master story tellers bring the best in tales of horror.

### Never Fear
Shh… Something's Coming…

### Never Fear – Phobias
Everyone Fears Something

### Never Fear - Christmas Terrors
He Sees You When You're Sleeping…

### Never Fear - The Tarot
Do You Really Want To Know…

### Never Fear – Apocalypse
The End is Near…

**RT Booklovers Presents: The Haunted West**


Written especially for RT Booklovers, best-selling and award-winning authors Diana Gabaldon, Heather Graham, Virginia Henley, Kat Martin, Katherine Neville, Bobbi Smith, Tina Wainscott, Tina DeSalvo and more... take you on a time-traveling, spellbinding journey through America's sprawling West.


**The Haunted West**, Volume 1


**The Haunted West**, Volume 2

## Romantic Times: Vegas

The Excelsior Hotel and Casino.in Las Vegas is the setting of these magical stories of romance. For decades the towering hotel has been the subject of incredible stories and rumors.  Bestselling authors, Christina Skye, Heather Graham, Tina DeSalvo and a story by the Lady of Barrow, Kathryn Falk will take you deep into the heart of those, in the past, present and future... who roam the halls of the Excelsior in search of that perfect love.

### Volume 1

### Volume 2

### Volume 3

## Heather Graham's Christmas Treasures

## Heather Graham's Haunted Treasures

Presented together for the first time, New York Times Bestselling Author, Heather Graham brings back three out-of-print Christmas classics that are sure to inspire, amaze, and warm your heart.

**Heather Graham's Christmas Treasures** also available in **Invoke Books Dyslexic Friendly**

New York Times Bestselling Author, Heather Graham brings back three tales of paranormal love and adventure.

## The Third Hour

*Winner of the USA Best Book Award - Thrillers*

The Third Hour is an original spin on the religious-thriller genre, incorporating elements of science fiction along with the religious angle. Its strength lies in this originality, combined with an interesting take on real historical figures, who are made a part of the experiment at the heart of the novel.

## Ripper – A Love Story

Prince Edward Albert Victor, The Duke of Clarence is Queen Victoria's favorite grandson and the most eligible bachelor in England. Coren Butler has captured his heart in the perfect Cinderella story. A dream come true. Then the nightmare begins.

## Uncharted Worlds: Xeno Encounters

Uncharted Worlds—an exciting new speculative fiction series featuring bestselling and award-winning authors. Ten mind-boggling adventures include tales of ancient aliens, other worlds, and imagined futures.

# On Two Fronts

*IBPA Silver Medal Best Non-Fiction Award Winner*

When two unlikely friends are separated by war, they must learn to cope with the effect it will have on their lives, their futures, and their relationship.

## Bad Attitude/Diamond in the Rough

**Bad Attitude** Meet bad boy, undercover state trooper Reid Cameron. Meet Polly Sweet, the woman who is about to be his downfall. In order to catch a jewel thief, Cameron wants to use Polly's house, and he comes up with a plan, whereby they play at being lovers. But when the first play-acted kiss happens, neither one is ready for the feelings that kiss ignites or for the consequences that ensue.

Has this bad boy finally met his match? How Bad is Too Bad?

Diamond In The Rough-Detective Dan Murdock is on a dangerous stakeout, when advice columnist, Millie Gordon unwittingly shows up on the scene, putting them both in danger. To save her from possibly being shot when the mobsters arrive, Murdock jumps into Millie's car and throws himself over her to protect her, little realizing that the real danger starts when their bodies come together.

Romance and action are the name of the game in this two-in-one duo from bestselling author Doris Parmett

## Calendar Girl

Fate, it seems, has derailed destiny... and found a love for all time.
Tina Wainscott weaves a tale you'll not soon forget.

# Family

Matthew Costello's widely acclaimed post-apocalyptic thriller, comes to it's amazing conclusion.

# Treasures and Pleasures

A Collection of Romantic Novellas from the bestselling author Bobbi Smith.

## Shadows in the Big Easy

Bouchercon Presents stories by up and coming Teen Writing Contest winners in this mystery anthology.

## Stop Saying Yes – Negotiate!

Stop Saying Yes - Negotiate! is the perfect "on the go" guide for all negotiations. Fortune 500 Companies world-wide send out their teams of negotiators with copies tucked away in briefcases and notebooks... maybe you should too?

## Do You Want To Be An Actor?


101 Answers To Your Questions About Breaking Into The Biz from people who know, Casting Directors, Producers, Directors and Agents tell it like it is.

## Zodiac Lovers Series

In this series of romantic, gay, paranormal stories tales of love lost, love found, and love to last for eternity will fill your heart with awe and your eyes with tears.

**Zodiac Lovers 1**: Aquarius, Pisces, Aries

**Zodiac Lovers 2**: Taurus, Gemini, Cancer

**Zodiac Lovers 3**: Leo, Virgo, Libra

**Zodiac Lovers 4**: Scorpio, Sagittarius, Capricorn

**Zodiac Lovers 5**: Cetus, Ophiuchus

www.ingramcontent.com/pod-product-compliance
Lightning Source LLC
Chambersburg PA
CBHW071307130626
46556CB00004B/1507